STARS OF SPRING

by

ANNE HAMPSON

HARLEQUIN — BOOKS

TORONTO   •   WINNIPEG

First published in 1971 by Mills & Boon Limited,
17 - 19 Foley Street, London, England

SBN 373-01551-8

Harlequin Canadian edition published December, 1971
Harlequin U.S. edition published March, 1972

Printed in Canada

1551

CHAPTER ONE

Conscious of being watched, the child glanced up. A swift mischievous grin transformed her angelic features and a smile of tender amusement rose to Joanne's lips. Following the direction of her gaze, the man stared through the window, watching the child as she disappeared round the corner of the house. His cool dark eyes flickered to Joanne . . . and to her left hand. It lay in her lap, half covered by the folds of her skirt.

'A relative of yours?' His voice held the lazy affectation of boredom; clearly the inquiry was a gesture of politeness and Joanne replied in tones of crisp formality, for in one brief hour the arrogant Dom Manoel Alvares had aroused in her a dislike so intense that she no longer made any effort to disguise it.

'Yes, she's a relative. Glee is my—'

'Mummy, I'm hungry!' Like a small hurricane she entered, tossed her small satchel on to the couch, and stood regarding the visitor with interest for some moments, noting the sign of disapproval as his eyes moved from her animated little face to the satchel flung against the cushions.

'What were you doing out there in the garden?' How quickly she grew, thought Joanne rather sadly. Glee would be six in less than two months' time.

'Burying a worm. It got itself in the sunshine, and it hurts it if you don't help it to get back under the soil again quickly.' Her chestnut hair – so like Joanne's – had been neatly plaited and held with two pretty blue ribbons, but it now fell untidily on to her shoulders, and she had one ribbon in her hand. Her grandmother had always declared it would be a miracle if ever Glee came home without having lost anything. Her large, almond-shaped eyes, so soft and grey, were still fixed on the formidable stranger, but he was looking at Joanne with a mingling of puzzlement and disbelief.

5

'Are you the man who wants to buy Mummy's farm?' asked Glee, without any trace of shyness. 'She won't sell it to you because we're going to live in it ourselves.'

'Glee dear,' put in Joanne hastily, 'hang up your satchel and then go to the kitchen. Auntie Chris will give you something to eat.'

Obediently she left the room, dragging her satchel along behind her.

'I must apologize.' Dom Manoel's voice carried an unmistakable note of censure. 'Evidently I should be addressing you as *Mrs.* Barrie. Why didn't you correct me?'

'It's of no importance.' Why waste time explaining when her one desire was to be rid of this objectionable foreigner who had spent the last hour trying to force her to part with her property? Deliberately she glanced at the clock; the action produced no visible change in his expression, yet Joanne sensed a sudden tightening of his mouth.

'You didn't say anything about farming the land yourself,' he began in some perplexity. 'If that were the reason for your refusal of my offer then why couldn't you say so?'

Her chin lifted at his tone, and a sparkle entered her eyes. What an arrogant voice – and it was made to sound more arrogant still by the slight accent and the emphasis he put on certain words.

'I didn't feel obliged to inform you as to my future plans,' she replied frigidly. 'What I choose to do with the farm is entirely my own affair.'

His dark eyes glinted dangerously, but he maintained a perfectly unmoved composure. He would rarely lose his temper, Joanne concluded – and yet she felt this quiet control could be far more unpleasant than any violent show of emotion – were one to find oneself in his power.

'Your husband – is he willing to leave his work here, and move to Portugal?'

She hesitated, then gave a shrug of resignation.

'I have no husband. I've never been—'

'Your pardon, Mrs. Barrie; I'm sorry. You're so young to be widowed, and left with a small child—' Pausing, he regarded her with renewed perplexity. 'You must have been very young indeed when your little girl was born?'

A question ... which she decided not to answer, and after a moment or two he stirred, then leant back in his chair. Joanne frowned. He was making himself more comfortable instead of preparing to leave.

'You can't possibly farm this land alone,' he stated firmly, adding that, in view of her misfortune in losing her husband, he would again increase his offer. He paused, this time to make a mental calculation, and before he could continue Joanne said, on a definite note of finality,

'My mind's made up, Dom Manoel, I'm not selling the farm.' She glanced coldly at him. 'You've managed without the land all this time, so it can't be of such vital importance to you.'

A gesture of his hands betrayed his impatience. His lean aristocratic features became set in lines that gave evidence of his acute distaste for his task. Nevertheless, he persevered.

'Originally it formed part of the Solar de Alvares estate. Naturally it is my desire to purchase it.'

Joanne lapsed into thoughtful silence, wondering what this farm was like, this farm in the lovely Douro district of Portugal. It had been left to her by a great-aunt, Dona Amelia Lucena, an eccentric who, having quarrelled with all her relatives in Portugal, left the property to the youngest child of her niece, Mrs. Barrie, whom she had never even met.

What was his house like? – the Solar de Alvares? From what her grandmother used to tell her Joanne felt it must be very grand. A great *palacete*, a patrician of rare line and beauty, reclining gracefully in the sun, spread out on a wide spur of the rolling hills above the Douro valley, with the purple richness of the vineyards pressing right up to the edge of its vast park. Its main façade, her grandmother had said, was flanked by two massive granite towers, and its grounds were a paradise of spreading lawns and statuary, of flower borders and ornamental water gardens.

7

And close by was the farm. Minute by comparison to the vast Alvares estate, it had been appropriated to a descendant of Nuno Alvares more than a hundred and fifty years ago, and had, therefore, become separated from the main estate.

Immediately on inheriting the property Joanne had been approached by a firm of solicitors engaged by Dom Manoel to make her an offer for it. In ordinary circumstances she would willingly have sold the farm, but a few months prior to her inheriting it events had occurred which were later to influence her, and make her exceedingly thankful that a means of livelihood had so opportunely presented itself.

On the failure of the solicitors to purchase the property Dom Manoel had decided to come to England himself, confident of persuading Joanne to sell. Judging by the way in which he had received her decision she felt sure no one had ever before had the courage to oppose his will.

He now moved impatiently and she looked up.

'There isn't anything more to say on the matter. I'm not selling my property.'

The compression of his lips portrayed his anger. Joanne was suddenly curious to read his thoughts. That he disliked her was plain enough; he also considered her to be both foolish and stubborn. His offer was good, and Joanne fell to wondering whether, had he not been so arrogant and sure of himself immediately on meeting her, she would have obliged and let him have the land he so greatly desired.

'This idea of farming it alone,' he said imperiously. 'You're just not capable!'

'Certainly I am!' One could do most things, when necessity drove. And it was of vital necessity that she make a living for herself and Glee.

'Ridiculous! You don't know what state the place is in. You couldn't possibly occupy the house – and as for the land, well, it's been neglected for years.'

Joanne smiled faintly at this ruse. Did he believe for one moment that she would be influenced by that kind of talk?

'If it's in such a dilapidated state, then why have you

made me so generous an offer?' she asked, her grey eyes wide and challenging.

'If I buy this property from you the house will be demolished. I'm interested only in the land; I want it back where it belongs.'

'I'm sorry to disappoint you,' and she added, in tones less cold, 'I must farm it, Dom Manoel, for I have no other means of making a living.'

He frowned at that and for a moment Joanne expected to be questioned as to her financial position. However, he thought better of it and all he said was,

'You'll never make a living out of this farm.'

'I can try.'

His dark eyes flashed, then roved her contemptuously.

'You'll fail. Labour is not easy in this area – even if you could afford it,' he added, bringing a hint of angry colour to her face. 'No, it's far better for you to accept my offer and find some small business for yourself in your own country.'

Her flush deepened. Who did he think he was? Let him keep his orders for the poor labourers who had the misfortune to work in his vineyards! She stood up, and waited in an attitude of impatience for him to do the same. His eyes seared into her and she wondered what sort of danger that expression would portend to anyone subordinate to his authority.

Presently he rose, and against her will she admitted to being profoundly impressed by the sort of magnificent aloofness with which he held himself. So tall and lean, with the typical dark complexion of the Alvares family and the widow's peak cutting low into his brow, he seemed to typify some great mediaeval overlord, and Joanne could almost see his lackeys cringing before his august and overpowering presence.

Well, for once he had met his match, she mused with extreme satisfaction. And if she ever did come to sell the farm, the haughty Dom Manoel would be the last person to whom she would give the option of buying.

'I'm afraid I have work to do,' she said without any effort at politeness.

But he did not leave immediately, instead he put to her a proposition that not only increased her anger and indignation, but also strengthened her determination to make an outstanding success of her farm.

He drove away in the taxi which had been waiting, and with a deep sigh of relief Joanne went into the kitchen where her sister was busy feeding sandwiches to Glee.

'I don't like that man,' submitted Glee, chewing vigorously. She had an attractive little turned-up nose and it went higher into the air as she added, 'He's a snob.'

'Devastatingly handsome, though.' Chris put a couple more sandwiches before the child and then eyed Joanne questioningly. 'How did you go on? Is he a snob, as this little brat says?'

'Snob's a mild word.' She glanced at Glee, her eyes resting on her long slender fingers as she began to pick out the meat from between two pieces of bread. 'He was as mad as could be about my decision to retain the property. Kept on increasing his offer—' She broke off, laughing. 'He thought I was a widow, so he very magnanimously increased his offer again.'

'A widow?' Chris blinked at her. 'Why should he think that?'

With a slight gesture of her head Joanne indicated Glee, who appeared to be completely absorbed in her food.

'He reached the conclusion that Glee was mine.'

Chris glanced from one to the other.

'That's understandable – though you don't look old enough.' She gave her attention to Glee, telling her sternly to eat her bread. 'That doesn't explain why he should think you're a widow?' she added on a puzzled note. Joanne explained what had happened and Chris said she supposed Joanne had put him right about the matter.

Joanne shook her head.

'I couldn't be bothered. I wanted to get rid of him.'

'But—' Chris stared – 'he took it for granted you were a

widow – and you let him believe it?'

'What does it matter? I'll never see him again.'

'You might; he'll be your nearest neighbour.'

'His lands are too vast for him ever to come into contact with me.'

'I still think you should have told him the truth.' Chris frowned and shook her head. 'It was a pity she ever began calling you M—' Joanne raised a hand, for Glee now listened with interest, the food on her plate forgotten. The conversation between Joanne and Chris followed other lines until, about ten minutes later, one of Glee's little friends called to see if she were going out to play.

'Keep to the garden,' Joanne said, wiping the crumbs off Glee's chin with a handkerchief. 'You mustn't go out on to the road.'

'No, we won't.' A roguish light appeared in those grey eyes which at times could be so serious, and even sad. 'If you can't find me I won't be out in the road, but only hiding in the bushes.'

Joanne regarded her sternly.

'Just you play where I can see you.'

'Okay,' returned Glee cheerfully, and disappeared into the garden.

'No wonder they called her Glee,' remarked Chris a few minutes later as, having made a cup of tea, she sat with Joanne at the kitchen table watching the two children through the window. 'She laughed almost from being born – do you remember?'

Joanne nodded, thinking of the thrill she had experienced at becoming an aunt. It had given her a feeling of importance, for she was only eighteen when Glee was born.

Two years later Glee's mother died and, unable to settle, Roger had taken a post abroad, bringing his daughter home to be cared for by his mother and sisters. When the child cried for her mother it was always Joanne who took her up, holding her tenderly and comforting her. No one else could soothe her in this way and it was soon apparent that Glee was beginning to identify Joanne with her mother. And as the child's happiness was the sole concern of them all, the habit of referring to Joanne as Mummy was never checked. As time went on it became more and more difficult to do anything about it, for although Glee knew Joanne was her aunt she stubbornly refused to call her anything else but Mummy.

'This is going to cause you some trouble,' Mrs. Barrie had warned. 'We should make her call you Aunt.'

'It's too late—' Joanne shook her head. 'It would be quite impossible now.'

'But people who don't know you . . . .'

Joanne had only laughed, and Chris had jokingly suggested she wear a wedding ring.

'Don't be so frivolous about it,' Mrs. Barrie said angrily. 'A wedding ring would spoil Joanne's chances of getting married.'

'So will the fact of Glee's calling her Mummy. Nice young men fight shy of girls with babies who came in by the back door.'

'Really, Chris!' protested Mrs. Barrie. 'These modern expressions are so indelicate!'

'That's not a particularly modern expression,' submitted Chris. She was laughing at her mother's look of distaste, and so was Joanne. Mrs. Barrie gave up, but added in a deeply troubled tone,

'Much as I've grown to love Glee, I do wish Roger would come and take her away, because if he doesn't I can foresee a great deal of embarrassment for you, Joanne dear.'

But she did not live to witness any embarrassment Joanne might suffer, and only a month after her death Roger returned to England – bringing his new wife with him. Mavis, though willing to take the child, was clearly not over-enthusiastic about the idea. Joanne was quick to sense her reluctance; she felt deeply troubled about the child's future and offered to keep her.

Roger's relief was apparent, but he obviously felt he should make some sort of protest.

'You can't. Now Mother's gone who is there to look after

her while you're at work?'

'We're managing now,' she pointed out. 'Chris is always in when Glee comes from school.'

'For the present, yes, but only because she and Miles are living here—'

'We shan't be getting a house of our own yet,' Chris had put in, agreeing with Joanne that the lack of enthusiasm in both her father and stepmother spelt unhappiness for Glee. The upheaval of being removed from those she had grown to love would be sufficient to cause some psychological unbalance for a time, but to go to people who had little or no interest in her would be disastrous.

As neither Roger nor his wife made any further protests it was agreed that Glee should remain with her two aunts, and Roger would continue to pay for her keep and her clothes. But even before the arrival of Mavis's first child Roger had written to say that, as he could no longer afford the money for Glee, she would have to come and live with him and Mavis.

'They don't really want her,' said Chris angrily. 'Don't you see, they know very well we won't part with her, and this is just a way of getting out of paying!'

Although Joanne herself was angry, she could understand her brother's difficulty, for he did not earn a high salary. And so it was agreed that he should be relieved of the burden of his child's keep.

It would not have mattered very much, for Chris and her husband contributed towards the expenses of the house, and Joanne herself earned a fairly good salary as assistant in the bank, but a few months ago Miles had been offered a post in Scotland. He was already working there, and looking for a house. Chris and Miles had offered to take Glee, and that seemed the only sensible way out of Joanne's difficulty. Joanne knew she would feel the loss acutely, but believed Glee would be given a far better chance in life if she were brought up with Chris and Miles. However, they had reckoned without Glee, who at first merely raised a strong objection to the idea, but later, when it seemed she would be forced to leave her beloved Joanne had, after a bout of un-controllable weeping, turned right in on herself and scarcely spoken a word to any of them for more than two days.

'Leave her,' said Miles, though in deeply troubled tones. 'She'll become used to the idea.'

'I can't—' Joanne shook her head determinedly. 'It's no use, Miles, she'll have to stay with me.' And it was amazing how relieved she felt on making the decision. To have parted with Glee, even though she would see her at holiday times, was something on which Joanne had not allowed her thoughts to dwell.

But life was to be a struggle, and Miles suggested that, until he managed to find a house, Chris should remain with Joanne. Then the letter arrived informing Joanne of her inheritance. She and Glee would go to Portugal and Joanne would become a farmer.

'It solves all my problems,' she had said. 'There'll be no need to pay someone to mind Glee during the school holidays – and I'm sure I can make enough to keep us both.'

Miles was sceptical, and also angry that Joanne, at so young an age, had the responsibility of a child who was not her own. Glee ought to be sent back to her father, he had said.

'Send Glee away?' Joanne exclaimed, staring at him. 'You really mean that?'

He shook his head resignedly.

'No, Joanne, I don't. But what trouble she caused when she decided to put in an appearance!' And he added, without any apparent reason for it, 'She'll cause a good deal more, I'm thinking, before she grows up and finds herself a husband.'

'How can you say so? Why should she?'

'You? – Aren't you wanting to get married?'

Joanne shrugged.

'If someone loves me he'll take Glee as well,' was all she said, and the matter of Glee and her future was dropped. Miles and Chris became resigned to the idea of Joanne's going to Portugal to farm her land, to grow maize and grapes, and enough food for her own and her young niece's requirements.

The children's high-pitched chatter brought Joanne back; she saw her sister's expression and laughed ruefully.

'I was miles away,' she owned.

'In Portugal?'

'Partly.'

'Tell me all about this man whom our outspoken Glee calls a snob?'

Joanne related what had happened, and by the time she had finished a troubled frown had settled on Chris's brow.

'You don't believe him about the state of the farm?'

'Certainly not. It was a ruse to get me to sell.'

'Perhaps you're right ... nevertheless, don't you think you should make some inquiries before you go?'

'I'm quite sure the house will be fit to live in,' Joanne stated confidently. And then she went on to tell her sister of Dom Manoel's final offer. 'Apparently he has in his care two children of his sister's. She's a widow and has been in hospital for some time. Dom Manoel thinks the children's English should be improved, so he's offered me the post of instructress to them. He says I can take Glee with me.'

Chris's eyes flickered.

'He did? He must want that land badly. Still, I think his offer was generous, don't you?'

Joanne's mouth tightened.

'The offer was put forward as an inducement for me to sell,' she retorted, and Chris had to smile.

'Obviously you don't intend giving him the benefit of the doubt.'

'There is no doubt. He wants the land and he'll go to any lengths to get it.'

Chris looked at her sister thoughtfully.

'If you did sell out to him you might be able to buy some sort of a business—'

'Exactly what he suggested. No, Chris, I'm quite determined to try my hand at farming. He says I'll have difficulty in obtaining labour, but I wouldn't dream of taking his word for that. And if I can get one or two good men I'll soon show the high and mighty Dom Manoel that I can make a success of the farm.'

'Well, knowing you, I daresay you'll succeed . . . if it's all as you're expecting it to be, that is.' Chris paused and then added, as the thought occurred to her, 'Should it be that the house and lands are in a bad state, and you really can do nothing with them, then you could still take advantage of his offer, I suppose? – could work for him, I mean?'

'I should think so – but I shan't have to.'

Something else crossed Chris's mind.

'Probably not, but if you do want to work for him you'll be grateful for his assumption that you're married.'

Joanne glanced up quickly, her teacup poised half-way to her mouth.

'What do you mean?'

'He'd be unlikely to employ you were he to think Glee were illegitimate.'

'Why?' Joanne frowned uncomprehendingly.

'Haven't you heard Grandmother speak about the un-sullied house of Alvares?' she queried with a laugh.

'I still don't understand. What did Gran say about the house of Alvares?'

'It's their proud boast that no illegitimate child has ever contaminated the illustrious threshold of the Solar de Alvares!'

Joanne's eyes darkened with contempt.

'That sort of boast is not difficult to associate with Dom Manoel,' she scoffed, adding, 'I wonder how they can be so sure of a thing like that?' Chris remained silent and the light of indignation entered Joanne's wide grey eyes. 'Anyway, Glee's not illegitimate; and were I forced to accept his offer of work – which I never shall be,' she added incon-sistently, 'then I'd naturally tell him the truth about Glee.'

'That she's your brother's child?'

'Of course.'

Thoughtfully Chris shook her head.

'It wouldn't sound convincing.'

'The truth must sound convincing!'

'It should do, I admit, but . . . I wouldn't advise it, some-how,' Chris murmured and, when Joanne looked inquiringly at her, 'He doesn't appear to be the sort of person who'd believe you, especially as you've told him you've been married.'

'I haven't told him I've been married.'

'Allowed him to believe you have, then – and that Glee is yours.' Chris shook her head again, more firmly this time. 'If things do go wrong, and you feel like taking advantage of his offer, then leave it as it is. It'll be much simpler than trying to explain, for I'm sure he won't believe you. You see, you've complicated matters by not correcting him immediately he jumped to the wrong conclusions.'

'Perhaps you're right, Joanne conceded after a little thought. 'Still, it's not important, because if I don't make a go of the farm we'll come back home.' What would there be for them? She pondered, frowning. The house was to be sold and the money shared between Roger and the two girls. With her share Joanne hoped to carry on until the farm began to pay, but should anything go wrong, and the capital were lost, she would have no alternative but to sell out and use the money to re-establish herself in England. Perhaps, she thought with a sudden hint of dejection, she would in the end be compelled to buy a small business as Dom Manoel had suggested. As Joanne could think of nothing more dull and uninspiring than spending eight hours a day behind a shop counter she dismissed the possibility of failure and said, with a lightening of her spirits, 'Such an eventuality won't occur, though, because I'm quite sure I'll make a great success of the farm.'

CHAPTER TWO

THE grapes had ripened to their full maturity and into Dom Manoel's vineyards swarmed an army of extra helpers — men, women and children, dancing and skipping along to the accompaniment of mandolins, pipes and guitars. They came from the neighbouring villages, to harvest and tread the grapes, for it was early October and in the Douro valley the vintage had begun.

Joanne stood by the farmhouse door, gazing pensively down to where the people were working, picking the grapes from the low bushes which grew on the narrow, hand-cut terraces running like the seats of some gigantic amphitheatre up the precipitous sides of the valley. For as far as she could see the lands belonged to Dom Manoel, but the vineyards formed only a part of the vast Quinta of Alvares.

'What are they going to do with all those grapes?' Glee came from the house and stood by Joanne. 'Are they going to sell them in shops? Who'd buy such a lot as that? Why didn't our grapes grow? Didn't you do it right?'

A reluctant smile broke over Joanne's pale face, and she tried not to reveal her dejection as she said,

'Which question would you like me to answer first?'

Glee looked up, and the inevitable grin appeared,

'I ask too many questions, don't I?'

'Who said that?'

'Auntie Chris.'

'Well, you wouldn't learn anything if you didn't ask questions.' She listened for a moment to the sound of laughter drifting up from the terraces below. 'The grapes are used to make wine.'

'O-oh, I like wine. Auntie Chris gave me some at Christmas. Can I have some next Christmas?'

Next Christmas. Joanne's mouth curved bitterly. The

way things were going they'd be lucky if, by the end of the year, there was any money left for food.

'You're too young for wine.'

'I had that much—' With her fingers Glee indicated the amount. 'I wanted some more, but Auntie Chris said no. Why didn't our grapes grow?' she asked again.

'I didn't do it right, Glee,' Joanne answered with a sigh, recalling how she had seen the bright, metallic sheen appear on Dom Manoel's vines. She hadn't realized it was the result of a very necessary spraying with a solution of sulphate of copper and lime. But in any case her vines had been neglected for years, and the farmhouse itself had been dilapidated when Joanne had first arrived. In fact, everything had turned out just as Dom Manoel had described. She had not been able to obtain labour ... but only because Dom Manoel employed every available strong man for miles around. Eventually Joanne had managed to get Luis, an elderly man who, having some grievance against Dom Manoel, had left his employ three months after Joanne took possession of Pendela Farm. He had been with her for less than a week when she realized that his labours would not be missed on the Alvares estate, nevertheless, she was grateful for what small help he did give, although his wages were now becoming a drain on her purse.

'Will they grow next year?'

'We might not be here next year,' said Joanne after a small hesitation. 'How would you like to go home again, to England?'

A little frown creased Glee's wide intelligent brow.

'I like it here, and I'm clever at school now, because I know lots of words— At first I didn't like it when I couldn't speak to the children, and they laughed at me, but I like it now. Don't you like it?'

'Very much, but it takes a lot of money to have the farm, Glee, and I haven't a lot of money.'

Glee considered this, and she turned to glance up at the house.

'Was it because you had to spend all your money for the

builders?'

'Yes, Glee, that's right. The builders took most of my money.' It had been foolish in the extreme to have the house renovated, but that stubborn streak in Joanne's nature prevented her from admitting defeat at this early stage. Yet through all her six months of struggle she harboured a grudge against Dom Manoel for what she had done. It was all very illogical, she had to admit, but she placed the entire blame on him for everything that had happened to her. Had he been more reasonable, adopted a less haughty and superior attitude, she would probably have listened to him. And even though she might not have taken his advice – and his offer – at the time, she most certainly would have done so immediately she saw the house and lands. Knowing that Dona Amelia had occupied the property until the time of her death, Joanne had naturally expected to find a reasonably comfortable house and a well-run farm. But Dona Amelia had lived the life of a recluse, occupying only one room, and allowing the farm lands to become overrun with weeds and the buildings to fall into disrepair.

Pride alone had caused Joanne to reject the idea of offering the property to Dom Manoel, and she had recklessly set about putting the house into some sort of order. It was now fairly comfortable inside, but it must still be an eyesore to her arrogant neighbour, whose magnificent manor house was much nearer than she had imagined. Her house and buildings marred his view, and Joanne was reasonable enough to own that, were she in Dom Manoel's position, she would make every effort to buy the farm and demolish the buildings.

'Here's Luis.' Glee's voice broke into Joanne's thoughts and she glanced across the courtyard to where her farm hand was approaching from the direction of the low building where they kept the hens. 'Why does he walk so slowly? Our teacher says you're lazy when you walk like that – but it might be because he's old.'

Luis was not very well – at least, he said he wasn't, and Joanne had no option but to let him go home. This had happened several times lately, and Joanne wondered whether it would be in order to stop his wages, but there was no one whom she could ask.

'I'll be in in the morning, Mrs. Barrie,' he promised, speaking in very broken English, and using the English form of title. Like Dom Manoel, Luis had assumed Glee was hers and so Joanne had not corrected his form of address. For the first time she began to feel the awkwardness of her position, and to remember those warning words of her mother's, '. . . I can foresee a great deal of embarrassment for you, Joanne dear.' Luis was speaking again, complaining of the pain in his back.

'I should rest it, then, Luis,' she advised, pushing a hand wearily through her hair. 'Do try to come in tomorrow — early, please.'

'I've said I'll be in,' he returned sulkily. 'I can't work with the backache, can I?'

'No, of course not.'

He ambled away, and had just disappeared into the trees on the edge of Joanne's land when Glee said,

'Here's Dom Manoel; he's coming through our field gate . . . and that nasty lady's with him.'

Joanne turned in surprise, then looked down at Glee in some puzzlement.

'What makes you say she's nasty?' Had even the child noticed the supercilious and condescending manner of the beautiful Rosa Fernandes? She was Dom Manoel's cousin, and Joanne had heard from Luis that she and Dom Manoel were to be married the following spring. 'How do you come to know her?'

'She asks me questions.'

'Asks you questions?' Joanne frowned down at her niece. 'When does she ask you these questions?'

'She stopped the car one day when I was coming home from school and asked me how old I was. I said I was six and a half.'

'What else did she ask you?' Joanne glanced up again; the couple had halted by the hedge and were surveying her nearest field. Rosa waved a hand and even from this distance it could be interpreted as a deprecating gesture.

'She asked me how old you were, and I said I didn't know. How old are you, Mummy?'

Joanne's lips compressed.

'Never mind. Did she ask you anything else?'

'She asked me if I had a daddy.'

'She—?' Joanne stared unbelievingly. Surely Dom Manoel had imparted to his fiancée the knowledge that she, Joanne, was a widow. 'What did you say to that?'

'I was going to say yes, and that he came to see me sometimes – when we were in England – but another car came up and she had to move. She stopped again farther along the road, but I ran home through the fields, because I didn't like her.'

The couple were walking on again. Mechanically Joanne glanced down at her left hand . . . and then, for some quite incomprehensible reason, she went into the house and, taking her mother's wedding ring from the box where she had always kept it, slipped it on to her finger. Then, after a glance in the mirror, she took up her brush and tidied her hair. The lovely grey eyes, large and wide, looked back at her, a most curious expression in their depths. This was not the first time Dom Manoel had paid her a visit; he had been twice before, and both times Rosa was with him. On each occasion Glee had been in bed . . . and on each occasion Rosa had asked some pointed questions about her. Why the interest? There seemed no explanation for it, but it troubled Joanne, especially now that Rosa had deliberately stopped her car in order to question the child herself.

'I think, Glee dear,' she said on returning to the front door, 'that perhaps you'd better go and play somewhere. Dom Manoel will want to speak to me privately.' She knew why he came; the interview would be unpleasant, but he would never persuade her to sell to him. For some weeks she had known she must consider selling out, but she was determined that Dom Manoel would never have the satisfaction of owning Pendela Farm.

'Play? Where can I play?' and, before Joanne could reply, 'I asked that lady if I could play with the two girls who live in the big house – their names are Filipa and Leonor – but she looked all stuck up, like Dom Manoel and said they weren't allowed to play with anyone like me.' She paused for a second to pick up a great fat spider that was climbing one of the decaying supports of the verandah, and Joanne transferred her gaze to the Solar de Alvares, standing on the green and undulating land above the valley, surrounded by beautiful formal gardens and enhanced even more by the distant backcloth of pine forest rising darkly against the vivid blue of the autumn sky. 'They're nicer than she is, though. I talked to them through the hedge once and I liked them. Filipa's seven and Leonor's nine, and they have lovely long hair and it's black and it shines. What shall I do with the spider?'

'Put it back where you found it.' Joanne's voice was sharper than she intended, but a sudden surge of anger rose within her, bringing a hint of colour to her cheeks. So Rosa Fernandes did not consider Glee good enough to play with the noble Alvares children? Such snobbery was out of date in England, and Joanne thought it was high time it disappeared here, too.

Glee looked up, puzzled, her eyes clouding momentarily.

'Are you cross?'

A smile instantly erased the anger from Joanne's face.

'Not with you, darling.' Dom Manoel and Rosa had almost reached them and Joanne did not press Glee to go and play. Perhaps her visitors would depart more quickly if the child remained, thought Joanne, pushing three chairs to the front of the verandah. She bade them 'good afternoon' unsmilingly, and invited them to sit down.

'Good afternoon, Mrs. Barrie.' Dom Manoel eyed the chair with some uncertainty, and Joanne could not quite make out whether he mistrusted its strength or whether he were afraid of some sort of contamination. Rosa certainly eyed her chair both with doubt and disdain, but as her

23

cousin at last decided to sit down she followed his example.

Glee stood there for a moment, examining them in turn, and then she sat down on the top step of the verandah.

'It doesn't run as quickly as ours at home—' She looked up at Joanne, her eyes twinkling with mischief. 'Do you think it's full of flies?' The spider was crawling up her arm and a shudder passed through Rosa's slender body.

'Put that down, Glee dear,' said Joanne on noticing the movement. 'It doesn't like being played with by such a giant as you.' As she spoke Joanne became conscious of Dom Manoel's eyes regarding her intently and she turned to meet his gaze. 'Glee should have been a boy,' she remarked, by way of explaining her niece's extraordinary behaviour.

Dom Manoel's dark eyes remained on her face for a moment and then travelled to that of the child sitting on the step. She was now holding her hand aloft, and the spider was suspended on its silver thread.

'With those eyes and that face and hair? That would be a waste indeed.'

The comment, so totally unexpected, brought Rosa's head up with a jerk. She looked at Glee as if seeing her for the first time, and then as she glanced at Joanne a strange and almost hostile light entered her beautiful brown eyes.

'My gran used to say I ought to be a boy.' Carefully Glee allowed the spider to settle on the support again. 'Have your little girls got a gran?' she inquired of Dom Manoel, adding, before he could speak, 'My gran's dead – she's gone to heaven.'

'Glee darling,' put in Joanne gently, 'just be quiet for a few minutes. Dom Manoel has something important to say to me.' A faint curve of his lips at that and Joanne added with the merest hint of defiance, 'I presume you've come to ask me, once again, to sell my farm?'

His dark eyes glinted and there was a swift return of his arrogance as he said, very softly,

'The time might come, Mrs. Barrie, when I shall lose interest in your property.'

A threat? She glanced quickly at him, her heart fluttering. Despite her firm intention of thwarting him, she now realized, not without a sense of shock, that at the back of her mind there had dwelt the sure conviction that, should she encounter difficulty in disposing of the farm to someone else, she could always sell out to Dom Manoel. To her dismay he seemed aware of her sudden fear, and in an effort to disillusion him she tossed her head and said lightly,

'As I am doing very well, Dom Manoel, your interest is of no importance to me.'

His black brows lifted a fraction.

'Your grapes failed, I believe?'

So he knew. And somehow Joanne was convinced he had known all along that they would fail, that he could have advised her about the spraying.

'Lack of experience on my part,' she admitted, contriving to retain her light and rather careless tone. 'I shall be more careful in future; I'm sure I shall have an excellent crop next year.'

'Will you, Mrs. Barrie—?'

'But you said we might not be here next year,' interrupted Glee, her wide brow puckering as she brought her gaze from the contemplation of the spider to her aunt's flushed face. 'You said we might go home to England.'

Although she fumbled for words that would bring about a quick recovery Joanne failed to find any, and the colour deepened in her cheeks. As if sensing she were the cause of her aunt's confusion Glee rose from the step and came to stand by her chair. Her arm went round Joanne's neck and she put her face on her shoulder. Rosa watched them intently, but Dom Manoel's attention was suddenly arrested by the man walking slowly across the field. Luis had come from the henhouse and he appeared to have something under his coat.

Dom Manoel's eyes narrowed.

'How long have you had that man working for you?' he demanded sharply, waving a hand in Luis's direction.

'Three months.'

'Three months, eh?' Without any explanation he rose and, taking long and easy strides, followed Luis, swiftly overtaking him.

'What's he doing?' Glee took hold of her aunt's hand, but she turned her head to watch Dom Manoel with childish interest. Absently she curled her fingers round Joanne's, then all at once she turned again, looking down at Joanne's hand in some puzzlement. 'Have you got a new ring, Mummy? You never used to wear it before. Where did you get it?'

Joanne drew her hand away, conscious of Rosa's searching scrutiny.

'I sometimes take it off, Glee – when I'm working hard – and I forgot to put it on again.' Glee's eyes widened in surprise and disbelief, but before she could say anything that could have embarrassed Joanne further, Rosa interposed in softly purring tones,

'You must have quite a lot of hard work to do, Mrs. Barrie, for this is the first time I've seen you wearing your wedding ring.'

'But then this is only the third time you've seen me, isn't it?' came the prompt rejoinder. Rosa's head tilted haughtily, but before she had time to retaliate Dom Manoel had returned, carrying a small basket in his hand.

'Eggs?' Joanne could only stare. 'Where did you get them?'

'Luis was the cleverest thief I've ever had the misfortune to employ,' he said, in tones of cold contempt. 'You'll do well to follow my example and dismiss him from your service.'

'That's impossible, for I can't get anyone else.' The admission came out before Joanne realized what she was saying, and she would have done anything to take it back, especially as Dom Manoel's quick intake of breath betrayed in no uncertain manner his total lack of patience with her.

'He stole them?' asked Glee awfully, putting out a finger to touch one of the eggs. Joanne relieved him of the basket, placing it on the table at the end of the verandah.

'I give him eggs every week, and vegetables.' She shook her head bewilderedly. 'He wouldn't steal from me – oh, I'm sure he wouldn't!'

'I've just taken the basket from him; he had it under his coat.' A slight pause, and then, 'He says he's going home because he's not well?'

'That's right. It's his back.'

'It was his chest when he worked for me. You'll stop him his wages, of course?'

Joanne shook her head, her eyes flickering to Rosa, who was watching Dom Manoel through faintly narrowed eyes.

'I haven't up till now. Is it permissible for me to do so?'

'Most certainly you must stop his money, otherwise he'll be evading his work all the time!' He stared down at her, and she saw the anger and impatience in his eyes. 'Be sensible,' he snapped, 'and accept my offer. I'll compensate you for what you've expended on the house—'

'But, Manoel, why should you do that?' interposed Rosa silkily. 'I'm sure Mrs. Barrie would not wish you to – well, to make her a present of the money, as it were.'

Dom Manoel's arrogant mouth tightened. It was plain that, even from his fianceé, he would not tolerate interference; Rosa flushed under his stare, and glanced away.

'Do you mean what Mummy paid for the builders?' inquired Glee innocently, adding with enchanting naïveté, 'It took nearly all her money, and I'll be glad if you pay it back to her because then she won't look so sad and worried—'

'Glee!' Crimson with embarrassment, Joanne looked sternly at her niece. 'It's very rude of you to interrupt our conversation. Now just be quiet!'

Glee's lips quivered; she lowered her head, turning away. Joanne frowned, remorse sweeping over her. Was the child crying?

'It seems to me,' commented Dom Manoel in a slightly softer tone, 'that you are in far greater difficulties than I realized – or than you would have me believe,' he added with a hint of censure. 'Now, I did offer you the post of instructress to my nieces, and if you care to take advantage of that offer, the vacancy still exists.'

How starched and formal, thought Joanne, still feeling acutely embarrassed by Glee's impulsive revelation. Did he ever unbend? Imagine being married to such a man! She tried to picture him in a gentle, tender mood ... and even in her despondency she could have laughed. The cold, punctiliously correct Dom Manoel Alvares would not even know the meaning of the word tenderness. Joanne's eyes strayed to Rosa's hand. No engagement ring there, but Luis was most emphatic in his assertion that they were to be married in the spring. Rosa lived at the Solar de Alvares – had done so since the death of her husband. She ran the house for him, and most efficient she was, according to Luis. But she hadn't taken at all to the idea of having Dom Manoel's nieces in the house. 'The master, though, he soon put her in her place,' Luis had added, a gleam of malice in his eyes and a note of satisfaction in his voice. 'She seems to like them now, but underneath, she would be glad to see them go.'

'I'm sure Mrs. Barrie would much prefer to return to her own country.' Rosa's soft and purring tones cut into Joanne's thoughts. She glanced towards her and Rosa added, surprisingly managing a smile, 'Aren't I right?'

Again Dom Manoel's mouth tightened, but it was not only that which caught Joanne's attention, for he was looking most oddly at Rosa, his eyes widening with a sudden perception that caused him to turn and examine Joanne's face as if seeing it for the first time. Flushing under his searching scrutiny, Joanne endeavoured to regain her composure by stating, in tones meant to be firm and final, that she had no intention either of accepting the post offered, or of returning to England. To her surprise Dom Manoel ignored this and said sharply,

'Mrs. Barrie will make her own decision, Rosa. She requires no prompting from you.'

'I wasn't prompting, Manoel,' protested Rosa. 'But surely you must see that Mrs. Barrie would feel very strange in a household like ours, and—' She stopped, biting her lip as

28

Dom Manoel raised his brows. 'In a household like yours,' she amended, throwing Joanne a glance of intense dislike, as if considering her to be responsible for the discomfiture she was experiencing.

Joanne's chin lifted and her grey eyes sparkled.

'As there isn't the remotest possibility of my entering your household,' she said in quivering tones, 'your anxiety on my account is quite misplaced!' Furious, she waited defensively for Dom Manoel's retaliation. Just let him open that arrogant mouth of his and she would instantly respond in kind! To her utter astonishment he appeared to understand, and to make allowances for her anger.

'You mustn't misinterpret Dona Rosa's words, Mrs. Barrie,' he said quietly, and a smile actually hovered fleeting on his lips. 'Presumably she was warning you that our way of life, and our customs, differ from those to which you have been used.'

'Dona Rosa was speaking to you, not to me,' she sharply reminded him. 'However, as I've said—' She broke off and looked up at him with a wide and half imploring gaze, her anger dissolving in response to the dropping of his own arrogant demeanour. 'As I've said so many times, Dom Manoel, I'm determined to keep my farm—'

'But you're not making it pay!' he cut in, once more exasperated. 'You can't live like this?' He flung out a hand, embracing the whole scene of neglect around him. 'This obstinacy is downright foolish!'

To her own surprise, Joanne received this with equanimity, taking not the least exception to his forthright statement. Perhaps, she thought, it was because what Dom Manoel said were true – she was obstinate, and she was foolish. A most puzzling sensation swept over her as she continued to meet his gaze . . . for he actually appeared to be anxious about her!

This could not be so, she decided quickly. No, her own unhappy state was a matter of indifference to him – how could it be otherwise, seeing that they were practically strangers? His interest rested solely with her property –

which he was quite determined to procure.

As she had so emphatically declared, she would never enter his household, so the idea of working for him was dismissed . . . but should she accept his offer for the farm?

Surprising herself by the question, Joanne nevertheless realized she was now in a mood to consider it seriously. Defeat had never been acceptable to her; over any difficulty she had risen – triumphant. But in the present case circumstances were different. She must admit defeat, and were she to accept Dom Manoel's offer it would certainly save her a great deal of trouble, for the finding of a suitable purchaser might be a lengthy business. As she wavered, her common sense battling against that stubborn streak in her nature, something occurred which instantly swept away all her hesitancy and made her more determined than ever not to let Dom Manoel have the farm.

Glee had been quietly hopping about on one leg; suddenly she overbalanced and instinctively clutched at Rosa's sleeve for support. Instead of giving her assistance, Rosa raised her hand and brought it down sharply on Glee's bare arm.

'You clumsy child!' The contact with Glee appeared to be what angered Rosa, and not the fact that Glee might have creased the sleeve of her dress. 'Don't you ever sit still?'

Dom Manoel turned his head, puzzled. Glee's action had escaped him, as also had Rosa's, for the girl had been wise enough to bring her hand down sideways, and so no loud slap was heard.

'What happened?' He glanced swiftly from Glee's bewildered face to that of Rosa. It was flushed with anger and she was looking at her sleeve as if it had been in contact with something unclean.

'That dreadful child! She deliberately pinched me—'

'Oh, you great big fibber! I never did!' Glee turned indignantly to Dom Manoel. 'Don't believe her; I only held her sleeve, so I wouldn't fall. She's a big—'

'Glee, that's quite enough.' Joanne's voice was firm, but not admonishing. 'Go into the house; I'll be with you directly.' She turned disdainfully to Dom Manoel. 'I'll bid you good afternoon,' she said in the stiff and formal tones so characteristic of his own manner of speaking. 'My time's valuable, and I've wasted far too much of it already.'

For one stunned moment he could only stare, and in spite of her ill-humour Joanne had an almost irrepressible desire to laugh. It was not difficult to read his thoughts. Never in his life had the lordly Dom Manoel Alvares been subjected to discourtesy such as this! It would perhaps rob him of a little of his conceit, mused Joanne with satisfaction, although she surmised from his changing expression that she would never be forgiven for showing such lack of respect, especially before an audience.

Rosa's dark face glowed with satisfaction as, rising, she moved towards the steps of the verandah.

'Your manners leave much to be desired, Mrs. Barrie,' she remarked smoothly, casting her a supercilious glance from under her thick silken lashes. 'Or is this incivility characteristic of the English?'

It was on the tip of Joanne's tongue to ask Rosa if her arrogance, and her deliberate unkindness to Glee, were characteristic of the Portuguese, but she refrained, her patience being quite beyond further discussion with proud, unsufferable people.

Dom Manoel had moved to Rosa's side, but his eyes never left Joanne's face as he said, very softly,

'You will come to regret your insulting behaviour, Mrs. Barrie.' And with that cryptic warning he bowed stiffly, stepped down from the verandah, and, with Rosa hurrying to keep pace with him, he strode away towards the great house standing on the rise.

For some reason, as she watched the departing figures, Joanne was overcome by a sense of foreboding. That warning ... was it really a threat? But what could he do? He would not deliberately damage her stock or her few crops ... but what else could he do to harm her? Perhaps she was allowing her imagination to run riot. Perhaps Dom Manoel, humiliated as he must have been, had said the first thing

31

that entered his head. Not that Joanne could imagine his ever doing a thing like that. She felt he would always carefully consider his words, and never say what he did not mean. As this conclusion brought her right back to the beginning, Joanne impatiently dismissed Dom Manoel from her thoughts and went inside to Glee. But Glee was not there; Joanne called and, receiving no answer, she went through the house and into the orchard. Again she called, but Glee was nowhere about. Frowning, Joanne returned to the house. Where could she be? Just as she was becoming uneasy, and trying to decide what to do, Glee came running across the field.

'They had a big row,' she submitted cheerfully, flopping down in a chair. 'She did hurt my arm — just look at that bruise!'

'Where have you been? I told you to come in here.'

'I went to get a herb to put on my arm — you can cure yourself with herbs. Did you know that?'

Joanne had to smile.

'A bruise, Glee, takes time to disappear, no matter what sort of herbal cure you give it.'

'I wish Dom Manoel had seen my bruise — then he'd have told her off more.'

Joanne's eyes flickered interestedly.

'How do you know Dom Manoel told her off?'

'I heard him. I was behind the hedge, finding my herb — it's got a wide leaf and a funny smell. Ana Maria at school said you rub it on if you have a pain — oh, yes, and then I heard Dom Manoel ask Dona Rosa what had happened — and do you know what she said? She told him again that I'd pinched her!'

'What did Dom Manoel say to that?'

'He said it might have been an accident, because I didn't seem like a naughty child.'

Joanne looked amazed.

'Did he indeed?' Had she misjudged him, then?

Glee nodded vigorously.

'Yes — well, Dona Rosa said you were rude, and Dom

Manoel said she was rude to you first, and he seemed very angry and said it was her fault that you wouldn't sell our farm. He said you were nearly selling it to him, but she upset everything by shouting at me.'

So she hadn't misjudged him. His concern was not with his fiancée's rudeness, but merely with the way that rudeness had affected his own plans.

'What did Dona Rosa say then?'

'I don't know, because they started talking in Portuguese.' Her eyes twinkled as she glanced up at her aunt. 'I ran along the hedge for a little way, just in case they began to speak English again, but they didn't.'

'Really, Glee, that was very wrong of you.'

'But you wanted to know what they said, didn't you? I understood a few words they were saying,' she added. 'Dom Manoel said you'd be glad to come to him and say you were sorry. Why should he say that?'

Joanne gazed pensively across to where the *solar* stood majestically on its low hill. The imposing seventeenth-century senhorial great house, with the autumn sun glinting on the carved armorial crest which occupied a large part of the colonnaded façade, had about it an essence of mediaeval grandeur and nobility that seemed to reflect the character of those who dwelt within its walls. Did warmth ever encompass those people? she mused. Did they ever experience the emotions of kindness and love? How could people be so cold, so unfeeling, and yet be happy? But their magnificent house, and the vast wealth of the *quinta*, seemed to be all that the great Dom Manoel and his fiancée required for their supreme contentment, concluded Joanne, her eyes wandering away from the house to where, sweeping down from its garden boundaries, lay part of the Douro valley. On its vine-clad sides scores of men, women and children worked, harvesting the grapes and transporting them in huge baskets to the *adegas* where the men would begin the treading, first stage in the wine-making process.

'He meant I should have to apologize for being rude to him,' Joanne submitted as Glee waited for her to speak.

'Will you apologize, Mummy?'

'Certainly not!'

'But you always say it's wrong to be rude, and if I'm rude you make me say I'm sorry.'

'Yes, Glee, that's quite true, but this is a little different.' And with that Joanne abruptly changed the subject, for judging by her niece's interrogating glance the conversation seemed likely to become involved.

CHAPTER THREE

WITH slow reluctant steps Joanne made her way past the lovely lake and proceeded towards the imposing front door of the Solar de Alvares. She paused, turning to view the tranquil scene from the top of the white marble steps. Fountains decorated with carved stonework and *azulejos* sprayed their sparkling water into small ponds; peacocks strutted on the lawns, proudly spreading their fans before the less spectacular swans and ducks and guinea fowl that stood preening themselves on the banks of the pools and lake.

The bell echoed through the hall and a moment later the door was opened by an elderly, white-haired butler; his eyes ran over her impassively when Joanne asked if she could see Dom Manoel Alvares.

'I haven't an appointment,' she added, 'but I think he'll see me.'

'Step inside, *senhora*, and I will find out for you.' Returning a little while later, he invited Joanne to follow him along the wide hall to a room at the far end. Then, standing aside for her to enter, he announced her in tones so stiff and formal that the slight nervousness she felt was immediately increased.

Dom Manoel sat at his desk, idly fingering a quill pen. He appeared to be totally absorbed in something he had written and Joanne was left standing there for several seconds before he at last raised his eyes from the pad before him. The delay in giving her his attention provided an opportunity for Joanne to glance around her, and she gave a little inward gasp at the luxury of the apartment. Although a study, it was also a sitting-room, with two large french windows opening on to a covered verandah and overlooking the steep-sided valley below. Persian rugs were strewn about the floor and an immense tapestry covered the whole of one wall. The other walls were hung with blue embossed satin, the couch and chairs were of blue damask and the two great cabinets were filled with rare Indian and Chinese porcelain.

'Sit down, Mrs. Barrie.' Negligently Dom Manoel flicked a finger, indicating a chair, and Joanne seated herself on the edge, aware that Dom Manoel's intention was to make her feel extremely uncomfortable before ever she made her request. That he knew what that request was became evident immediately she spoke, for apart from an indifferent flickering of his eyes he betrayed no emotion whatsoever. He was neither surprised by nor interested in what she had to say.

'So you've decided to sell your property?' Dom Manoel shrugged his broad shoulders. 'But why have you come to me, Mrs. Barrie? Can it be that you have failed elsewhere?'

No fool, the arrogant Dom Manoel Alvares. He was fully aware that the offer was made to him as a last resort.

'You were eager to buy my farm,' she reminded him, her heart sinking as, once again, he shrugged his shoulders.

'I was interested, certainly, but you refused to sell.' The pen was placed in its silver stand with a firm, deliberate movement. 'I'm no longer interested, Mrs. Barrie.' He glanced past her to the open window, and his attention appeared to be riveted on two white doves which had settled on the low wall of the verandah.

Joanne spread her hands helplessly. There was no time for pride now or for a stubborn refusal to admit defeat. The farm would never pay, even could she have procured the necessary labour for the efficient working of it. The soil was poor, having been so long neglected; the vines were old and the buildings practically falling apart. She had been a fool not to have approached Dom Manoel immediately on her arrival. Instead, because of a stupid pride, she had spent her last penny on trying to succeed – and now she had lost everything. For although she had advertised the property for over two months, no one was interested in buying so dilapidated a place.

True, one young man had called many times ... but Joanne knew by now that his interest was in her rather than the farm, for there was no mistaking those flattering glances which Ricardo Lopes invariably bestowed upon her.

'Dom Manoel,' Joanne murmured pleadingly, 'surely you will make me an offer.'

From under dark brows his eyes moved indifferently over her.

'I seem to remember making you several offers – excellent offers, Mrs. Barrie, that far exceeded the value of the land. I also warned you that you'd come to regret your insulting behaviour to me. Unless I'm mistaken you're already most bitterly regretting it.'

Joanne flushed. What arrogance and pomposity! What could Dona Rosa see in such a man? Was she attracted by his wealth? Joanne wondered, for there surely could be nothing else in which she was interested!

'I believed I could make a success of the farm,' she said, keeping her dislike of this man hidden only by the greatest effort. 'I find I've made a mistake – which after all can happen to anyone – and I now know I can't cope with the problems resulting from the previous neglect of the place.' She waited, but Dom Manoel merely leant back in his chair and lifted one lean brown hand to stifle a yawn. 'You won't make me an offer, then?'

'I'm no longer willing to buy your farm, Mrs. Barrie.'

'But what can I do?' she blurted out in sudden desperation. 'I haven't even enough money to take us back to England.'

'My dear Mrs. Barrie,' he said, quite unimpressed by her words, 'your financial difficulties are entirely your own affair – and, I should imagine, private.' Thrusting his hands in his pockets, he regarded her in silence for a moment and then added, 'In any case, I can't be expected to become involved. If through your own obstinacy and foolhardiness you've bankrupted yourself, it isn't any concern of mine.' He cocked her a glance, half amused, half interrogative. 'I think you'll agree with me about that?'

No answer. Joanne felt she hated him, and yet she could in a way understand his exploiting the situation. Several times she had snubbed him. To a man so used to respect, a man so steeped in his own superiority, her insults must have come as a blow which would not easily be forgotten – and probably never forgiven. This was his revenge; he had known all along that his chance would come, had guessed that, finally, she would have to approach him, begging him to take the farm— Begging? she would never beg. If someone would give her the price of the fare home she would sell. But even as she made these mental resolutions Joanne was seized with a sudden fear that however little she was prepared to accept, no customer would be forthcoming.

'Won't – won't you give me anything for it?' she whispered desperately. 'Surely you still want the land?'

A silence fell on the room; it seemed to Joanne that Dom Manoel was reluctant to reply to her question. Unwilling to lie, yet too proud to admit the truth. . . . Was that it? Impossible to tell, for his face was a mask, a mask of haughty indifference. With an easy, graceful movement he leant forward and rang the ornate little silver bell lying on his desk beside the blotter.

'I don't think there's any need for you to waste any more of your time,' he remarked in cool and even tones. 'If I remember correctly you did remind me that it was most valuable,' and, as the butler entered softly from the hall, 'Show Mrs. Barrie out, Diego, will you?'

The man stood there impassive, door in hand, and Joanne rose unsteadily to her feet. She seethed with anger at providing Dom Manoel with this opportunity for revenge. And yet what else could she have done? She'd been forced to approach him, and even though prepared for a rebuff she had felt confident of selling out to him in the end.

Without a word she followed the butler from the room, humiliated in a way never before known to her. The sooner she left this country the better, she decided, still choked with fury as she crossed to the field gate leading on to her own property. She would write to her brother for the money—But no, he wouldn't have it to spare. Chris would, though. Yes, she'd get in touch with her sister right away.

Her intention was never carried out, for by the very next post a letter arrived from Chris saying Miles had been unable to settle in his new job and they were leaving Scotland immediately.

'The expense of this upset has had pretty grim effects on our finances,' Chris added, and went on to say they would be living from hand to mouth for the next month or so until Miles managed to get himself fixed up in a post back in England.

Ricardo called that evening. Already they were on Christian name terms and after only the slightest hesitation she dejectedly related what had happened.

'Dom Manoel won't buy?' He frowned in puzzlement. 'But everyone knows how he's wanted this place. He even tried to buy it from Dona Amelia. It's most odd he's now refused to buy it from you.'

Disinclined to explain, Joanne changed the subject, asking Ricardo about his mother who, he had said, had been ill in bed but was now up and about again.

'Perhaps you'd like to visit her?' he suggested eagerly. 'She speaks a little English, so you'd be able to converse. She'd love to have someone new to talk to. Will you come?'

'Yes,' Joanne agreed after a slight hesitation. 'I don't see why not. I'll have to bring Glee, of course. It won't be too much for your mother, will it?'

Ricardo shook his head.

'She loves children; she has two grandchildren – my brother's boys. Henrique is just about Glee's age and Fernando's a year older.'

'They don't live around here?'

'They live in Lisbon, but my brother and his wife travel up often to see Mother.' He paused, glancing across the field as Glee came bounding towards the house. 'When will you come?'

'Whenever you like. This evening?'

'Better make it tomorrow evening, so I can give her a little warning.' Ricardo looked around as Glee made her whirlwind entry. Her face was flushed and she was breathless from running.

'Hello, Mr. Lopes! Oh, it's hot!' Glee flopped into a chair and wiped the perspiration from her forehead with her hand, leaving a smudge that made her look decidedly grubby.

'It's only hot because you've been running,' laughed Ricardo, reaching over to ruffle her hair. 'She's cute, this young daughter of yours?' His gaze returned to Joanne; he seemed puzzled and slightly uncertain. 'You must have been very young when she was born?'

The same question as Dom Manoel had once asked, but this time Joanne answered it.

'I was eighteen.'

'Eighteen!' he ejaculated, then instantly recovered himself, though there was a flush on his face as he added, 'So you're twenty-four. You're too young to be working your fingers to the bone on this place. The sooner you get rid of it the better.'

'I'm very much afraid I'll never get rid of it,' she said pensively. 'I'm thinking of trying to borrow the money to take us back to England.'

She watched Ricardo's changing expression, saw his handsome face cloud. Equally as dark as Dom Manoel, and with firm and well-defined features, he was, to Joanne, much more pleasant in appearance. For there was an attractive youthfulness about him, and he had an amiable expression which contrasted sharply with the severity of Dom Manoel's cold and aristocratic face. Did Dom Manoel ever laugh? Joanne wondered, and suddenly found herself trying to visualize what change such a possibility would produce. Chris had declared him to be handsome, despite his severity, and Joanne grudgingly had to admit that what her sister said was true, and still more grudgingly she owned to the fact that, should Dom Manoel ever relax those taut features, allowing humour or compassion to soften them, he would be just about the most breathtakingly attractive man she had ever met.

'Must you go back?' Ricardo's voice cut into her thoughts and almost angrily she shook them off, experiencing a faint disgust at the idea of wasting her time on the man whom she had come to dislike with an intensity she would never have believed possible.

'There's no means of my making a living here,' she returned flatly. 'I shouldn't have come in the first place.'

'I hate the idea of your going away.' He glanced at Glee as if wishing she weren't there. 'I'm getting to know you, Joanne, and – well, I might as well tell the truth. I like you very much.'

Absently Joanne shook her head.

'I like you too, Ricardo, but I can't stay here. At home I can easily get a job.'

'It's so awful thinking of your having to bring up Glee all on your own.' Again he looked at the child; she was listening with interest to all that was being said. 'Look, Joanne, I'll come back this evening, and perhaps we could have a talk?'

'There isn't anything to talk about.' She looked at him, her lovely eyes grave and faintly apologetic. 'We hardly know each other,' she reminded him gently.

'I've known you two months,' he objected. 'That's plenty long enough to fall in love.'

'Please, Ricardo, don't talk to me like this.'

'Are you in love with my mummy, Senhor Lopes?' interposed Glee, her eyes sparkling. 'If you get married can we stay here always?' she added, turning to Joanne. 'I don't want to go back to England.'

'I'm not thinking of getting married.' Joanne spoke sharply, and Glee, who had sat up straight on hearing Ricardo's words about love, instantly sank back again in her chair, acutely sensitive to the hint of anger in her aunt's voice.

'You've upset the child,' protested Ricardo, casting Joanne a glance of censure. Then, to Glee, 'Your mummy might change her mind and stay here. We'll have to try to persuade her.'

But Joanne firmly shook her head.

'We can't stay, Glee dear.' She spoke gently, smiling at Glee. 'As I told you, our money has all gone – and you can't buy food if you haven't any money, now can you?'

'Is it really as bad as that?' Ricardo spoke hesitantly, wondering if his blunt question would bring a frown of annoyance to Joanne's eyes. But she merely shook her head, giving him a faint smile.

'It's really as bad as that, Ricardo. I meant what I said when I spoke of having to borrow money in order to get back to England.' Why should she confide in him like this? Puzzled, Joanne looked straight at him, noting the shadowed brow, the pursed lips and the unmistakable anxiety in his dark eyes. An odd feeling swept over her and her puzzlement grew. Was this warmth in her being the first germ of love? Attractive as she was, Joanne had had her share of admirers, and consequently there had always been a ready escort to take her to a dance or a theatre, but no tender emotion had sprung from her friendships with these escorts. Never had she known the least pang of jealousy or regret when, eventually, they had found permanent girl-friends and she had lost the pleasure of their company.

Aware of Ricardo's curious stare, and inexplicably confused by it, Joanne hastily lowered her head, conscious of the colour rising in her cheeks.

'Don't make a decision just yet.' Ricardo's voice, low, persuasive, increased Joanne's uncertainty – and her confusion. It was impossible to make a firm, negative reply and to her utter astonishment she found herself saying she would try to manage for a little while on the money she was receiving from the man who bought her chickens and eggs. Bewildered by this pronouncement she glanced up ... and again that peculiar feeling assailed her. It *must* be the beginning of love, she decided, for there was a certain charm about Ricardo which she now realized had made itself felt at their very first meeting.

Should she go home, and so avoid becoming more deeply involved? If she stayed, and this friendship did develop into love then she would have to enlighten Ricardo as to her relationship to Glee, inform him that she was not a widow. That he would be glad she had never been married she did not doubt, but what did trouble her was whether he would be willing to take Glee on learning she was not hers. This question had remained with Joanne ever since her sister once remarked,

'When you do find a prospective husband, Joanne, it's more than likely he'll expect you to return Glee to her father.'

She would never do that, Joanne had firmly asserted. If the man didn't love her enough to take Glee as well, then she, Joanne, would consider his love not worth having.

'Do you mean we're not going home yet?' Glee asked, jerking Joanne back to the present and to the problem that had caused her thoughts to stray to that remark of her sister's.

'Not immediately,' she smiled, and the faces of both Glee and Ricardo cleared with miraculous suddenness.

The autumn evening was cool, yet soft, and with a strange translucent clarity of light that threw into relief the low wooded hills and the dark outline of pine forest beyond. Joanne sat on the verandah listening to the laughter of the children in the orchard at the side of the house. Glee's two little friends from school – Geraldo and Mariana – had begun coming up from the village to play at the farm, a circumstance for which Joanne was grateful, for it was not good for Glee to be so much with an adult. At home she had had her playmates, but for the first month or two here she had relied entirely on Joanne's company after coming from school each afternoon.

The children were speaking in Portuguese, but now and then Glee would have to resort to English even though it was quite lost on her young companions. What the conversation was Joanne did not know, but she heard Glee refer to her

43

'Uncle Ricardo'. A faint smile touched Joanne's lips, giving them a tenderness and enchanting beauty of which she was entirely unaware. Ricardo was devoting most of his energies to Glee, determined through her to make some advance in his relationship with Joanne.

'We went to see his mummy last night – she's a nice lady.' Immediately realizing the futility of this Glee tried to convey the message in Portuguese, and as Joanne could not understand a word she began dreamily to reflect on the visit to Senhora Isobel Lopes. Small and rather stout, she had the pleasant friendly manner of her son and welcomed Joanne with an embrace and a kiss on her cheek. Joanne could not make out if the reason for this was that Senhora Lopes was under the misapprehension that the affair had progressed further than was the case, or whether the rather effusive demonstration was the customary greeting in this particular part of Portugal.

The evening had passed pleasantly and, when looking at the clock, Joanne had realized it was after nine she gasped at the speed with which the time had flown.

'I must go; Glee will never be up for school in the morning!' she exclaimed, glancing apologetically at Senhora Lopes who was spreading her hands in a gesture meant as an invitation to remain a little while longer.

'Joanne will come again, Mother,' Ricardo said, speaking in English for the benefit of his visitors. 'Next time she and Glee must come for a meal.'

'Yes, that would be very nice,' agreed his mother, and then, 'See them home, Ricardo, right to the house, for it is dark and the road is so – so – what you say?' She looked rather helplessly at her son before turning to shake her head at Joanne.

'Rough and rocky,' he laughed, and added, 'Yes, I'll see them right to the door. I wouldn't think of leaving them to go home alone.'

He had taken Joanne's key and unlocked the door for her; Glee had raced into the house in her customary boisterous manner, despite the fact that she had been yawning all the way home . . . and before Joanne realized what was going to happen Ricardo had taken her in his arms and kissed her gently on the lips. He held her for a little while, and then kissed her again. She made no protest, but neither did she make any response. The way in which Ricardo received this was not known to her, as almost complete darkness prevailed all around them, and Ricardo's expression was hidden from her eyes.

'Good night, Joanne,' he whispered, close to her ear. 'Good night, and sleep well!' And with that he was gone, away into the gloom, and although she had felt his kiss for a long while afterwards, no real emotion touched her.

Deeply engrossed in these reflections Joanne was not aware of just when she ceased to hear the children's voices. But the deep cool silence eventually impressed itself upon her and she called out, at the same time rising from her chair and going round the side of the house in search of the children. They were along the lane, and all waved to her as she beckoned them to return to the garden. And then, round the bend in the lane came Dona Rosa's great car. Completely unperturbed, Joanne watched the children make for the side – Glee to the left and the village children to the right – subconsciously expecting Dona Rosa to slacken speed. But to her horror and incredulity Joanne saw the car leap forward, and at the same time swerve in Glee's direction. The silence was shattered by the screams of Geraldo and Mariana, as Glee's small body dropped to the ground.

Almost suffocated by the thudding of her heart, Joanne raced through the orchard and reached the lane just as Dona Rosa was languidly uncurling her slender body from the seat of the car. No hurry, no urgency . . . she did not care if Glee were dead! Hatred mingling with her terrible fear and dread, Joanne stooped and lifted Glee into her arms. A spasm passed through Glee's body; it seemed to release some spring within Joanne and she turned on Rosa, her eyes blazing.

'You—! You did it deliberately! You could easily have avoided her!'

Rosa's eyes widened in a sort of injured astonishment.

'You must be out of your mind,' she flashed indignantly. 'You believe I'd deliberately run a child down?'

'I saw it all. Not only did you accelerate, but you also swerved in Glee's direction. If – if you've killed her. . . .' All anger submerged beneath her fear, Joanne started to cry. 'You c-could have avoided her,' she quivered, looking helplessly at Rosa. 'You are taking her to the hospital?'

The dark girl's brows rose at this request.

'You insult me, then ask a favour? It was the stupid child's own fault – or perhaps I should say it was yours, as you don't seem to have the least idea of the way in which a child should be brought up. She makes an absolute nuisance of herself.'

Joanne scarcely heard. She asked again if Rosa were taking them to the hospital.

'There isn't much wrong with her. I'll telephone for the doctor when I get back to the Solar de Alvares. Put her to bed; she'll be all right in the morning.'

'But. . . .' Dazedly Joanne stood there, the apparently lifeless Glee in her arms, staring in disbelief at the icy indifference portrayed on Dona Rosa's beautiful face. 'You're – you're doing nothing about it?' She shook her head, still unable to comprehend such callous behaviour. 'You *must* take us to the hospital'

Dona Rosa walked towards the car, slid into the seat and pressed the ignition.

'Dom Manoel remarked on your insolence, Mrs. Barrie, but this presumptuous giving out of orders goes beyond all! Think yourself fortunate that I've agreed to ring the doctor.' And with that she let in the clutch and the car purred away, stirring up a cloud of dust on the road behind it.

The two children from the village began to follow Joanna as she made her slow progress towards the farm; tears were streaming down her face and her heart still raced with sickening speed.

'Go home, please,' she said, turning her head, and although they did not understand the words the children

46

grasped their meaning, for they obeyed at once, murmuring to themselves and to each other as they retraced their steps along the lane.

Glee was a dead weight in her arms and Joanne was stumbling by the time she reached the house. Blood came from some part of Glee's body and had penetrated Joanne's clothing; she felt it warm and sticky on her chest and arm. With trembling fear she laid Glee down on the bed and began to undress her. Her back was so greatly scratched and torn that it was evident she had been somehow pushed along the rough gravel-strewn road.

'How could she? – oh, how could anyone do this to a child?' Scarcely able to see for her tears, Joanne continued to take off Glee's clothing. At last she was undressed and Joanne could see the extent of her injuries. Although extensive, they did not appear to be serious, Joanne discovered with overwhelming relief. Nevertheless, Glee required immediate medical attention and, convinced that Dona Rosa would not trouble to phone the doctor, she carefully covered the unconscious child with a blanket and then determinedly took herself off to the Solar de Alvares. If Dona Rosa wouldn't help, then perhaps Dom Manoel would. And if he refused . . . if he should dare to refuse, thought Joanne, her eyes blazing, she would tell him exactly what she thought about him – and about his arrogant and heartless fiancée!

The bell clanged and Diego's dark face was a study as he opened the door. Apparently no one had ever dared treat the bell of Alvares in this disrespectful way before.

'I wish to speak to Dom Manoel Alvares,' Joanne snapped, giving him stare for stare. 'And it's urgent – so please tell him to see me right away!'

'*Senhora!*' He seemed about to collapse, so great was his surprise. 'You can't come here like this—'

'Where is he?' she demanded fiercely.

'In his room, working, so it's quite impossible—' Without further ado Joanne brushed past him and ran down the hall to the door at the far end. '*Senhora—*' The old man hurried along in her wake. 'You can't do this! What will Dom

Manoel say—?'

'I've already done it, so you can take yourself off! I intend to see Dom Manoel and no one is going to stop me!' She turned as she spoke and in that few seconds the door opened from the inside. Turning again with the intention of flinging herself through the door, Joanne literally fell into Dom Manoel's arms!

'Oh . . .' was all she could utter as she tilted her head to stare at him in dismay. There was no trace of understanding in his eyes; Rosa, then, had made no mention of the accident.

'What's the meaning of this, may I ask?' His hands still supported her as he looked over her head, putting the question to his butler.

'The *senhora* . . . she forced her way in, Dom Manoel.'

'Glee,' Joanne managed to stammer. 'She's – she's been knocked d-down and needs a doctor. . . .' A dreadful shuddering took possession of her. It must be reaction, she concluded, quite unable to keep still. Dom Manoel led her into the room, placing her with an odd gentleness on the couch by the fire.

'Now tell me, calmly, what has happened?'

'It's Glee—' She made an effort to rise but a firm hand on her shoulder kept her where she was. 'Oh, please—' And then to her utter dismay she burst into uncontrollable weeping.

'Where is your little girl?' Dom Manoel inquired softly.

'At home – on the bed, unconscious. I don't think she has any serious injury, but she's terribly grazed and bruised. I want you to get the doc— I mean, if you would please arrange for a doctor to come?' Again she made an effort to rise, and again the pressure of Dom Manoel's hand restrained her.

He looked across to where Diego was standing by the door.

'Have Pedro take the car to the farm. Go with him and bring the child here.' He glanced down at Joanne. 'Is the door locked?' and, when she shook her head, 'Where's the key?'

'On a hook in the kitchen – by the stove,' she added, becoming confused by the turn of events. This was so vastly different from what she had expected that she found speech exceedingly difficult. 'Glee's completely undressed. I must see to her myself.'

Joanne might not have spoken, for all the notice Dom Manoel took of her.

'Go quickly,' he instructed his butler. 'And before you come away see that the place is securely locked up. Mrs. Barrie and the child will not be returning there tonight, so you must also see that the animals are fed. Take one of the men with you.'

Diego inclined his head respectfully and said, in quiet, impassive tones,

'Will there be anything else?'

Dom Manoel frowned in puzzlement. 'Not that I know of.'

'The *senhora* . . . if she is to stay here . . .?'

'Ah, yes. Take Luisa. She must bring what the *senhora* will require for the night—' He broke off, his brow contracting sternly as Joanne made an attempt to interrupt. She immediately closed her mouth; she also relaxed under the firmness of his grip. No use trying to rise, and in any case she felt so shattered and weak that Dom Manoel's efficient management of the situation was an overwhelming relief. 'It doesn't matter about the child's clothes,' he went on, removing his stern gaze at last from Joanne's pallid face. 'We have plenty here that will fit her. Luisa will also see that the child is wrapped in a blanket – but you will carry her to the car, and hold her carefully till you get back here.'

Still very dazed by all that went on, Joanne continued to stare up at Dom Manoel. The tears had flowed freely, and automatically she rubbed her eyes with the back of her hand. And then, for the first time, she saw the hint of a smile touch that cold set mouth as Dom Manoel, reaching into his pocket, brought forth a handkerchief and dropped it into her lap. Diego had already left the room and Dom Manoel moved from Joanne's side to pick up the telephone. A few minutes later he was with her again, seated on a chair opposite to her and offering her a glass containing brandy.

'I'll be all right,' she murmured, shaking her head.

'Drink this.' So quiet his voice, but firmly commanding for all that; Joanne took the glass and held it to her lips. 'Stop trembling, my child – and stop worrying over your little girl. My orders willl be carried out promptly; she'll be here almost at once. The doctor's already on his way.' He paused and Joanne could only gape with admiration at the swift and orderly method with which Dom Manoel had set things moving – and without any visible sign of urgency or haste. He was speaking again, asking how the accident had occurred.

Initially, Joanne had meant to relate everything, but now she became guarded. Having had time to think, and in some measure to calm down, she perceived that Rosa would instantly deny the accusation, and that Dom Manoel would naturally take her word in preference to that of Joanne herself.

'The car ... it came round the bend, and the children – that is, two from the village, and Glee – were playing in the road. ...' Joanne tailed off, for although reluctant to say it was Rosa's car, she felt he must soon discover the truth.

'You allow your child to play in the road?'

A flush spread, and she found words more difficult than ever under that inquiring and faintly critical gaze.

'They were playing in the orchard at first,' was all she offered, and to her surprise Dom Manoel nodded understandingly.

'Our two have their moments of disobedience – but they're children, and can't always see that restrictions are for their own good.' He flicked a finger, indicating her drink, and Joanne took a sip from the glass. 'About this car? The driver offered to take the child to hospital, surely?' Dom Manoel added in some perplexity, and Joanne's heart gave a little lurch. How could she reply to such a question without

50

telling the whole story?

'The driver – the driver . . .'

'Yes?' he prompted softly. 'Do you know the driver?'

Perspiration began to dampen Joanne's forehead. Dom Manoel's face was stern and set; she felt with certainty that nothing would be gained by revealing the truth. He would never believe his fiancée capable of such callous behaviour, especially as he himself was obviously not nearly so heartless as one would deduce from his outward austerity of manner.

'No,' she murmured at length, deliberately avoiding his piercing gaze. 'No, Dom Manoel, I have no idea who the driver was.' Putting the glass to her lips, she took another drink of the brandy, and then she ventured to look up, for a profound silence had descended upon the room. Dom Manoel's dark eyes glittered, and Joanne involuntarily gave a shudder of apprehension.

'He drove on? – after knocking your child down?'

'The driver did stop—'

'Then why didn't he promptly take the child to hospital?'

'The driver didn't think Glee was badly hurt, and so—'

'The extent of the injuries has nothing to do with it!' He paused, eyeing Joanne in some perplexity. 'Didn't you ask him to take your little girl to hospital?'

Joanne swallowed, endeavouring to remove the dryness in her throat. She experienced a strange fear, wondering at Dom Manoel's reaction towards herself should he ever learn the truth. That he would condemn this deception she had no doubt, but after a little thought Joanne threw off her apprehension. She and Glee were here for one night only, and as Glee was at present too ill to talk, it was most unlikely he would ever come into possession of the real facts. For they would certainly never come from Dona Rosa herself.

'The driver was in a hurry,' she told him, hoping that would end the matter, but Dom Manoel asked again if Joanne had requested him to take Glee to hospital. 'Yes, I did,' she was forced to admit and Dom Manoel gave a sharp intake of his breath before he said, in tones so soft and dangerous that once again Joanne felt a shudder pass through her,

'He refused your request?'

Joanne nodded, searching for words, but at that moment the door opened and in walked Rosa. At the sight of Joanne sitting there, with the glass in her hand and Dom Manoel fairly glowering as he pondered over the news just imparted to him. Dona Rosa stopped abruptly, the colour slowly leaving her face.

'What – what is the matter?' she stammered, unsure of herself for the first time in her life. 'Is Mrs. Barrie ill?' Her attention was suddenly arrested by the handkerchief lying on Joanne's knee. Its presence there spoke for itself and Dona Rosa's eyes gleamed with an almost malevolent light.

'Some scoundrel's knocked down Mrs. Barrie's child,' he informed her harshly, 'and has driven off without even taking her to the hospital.'

Dona Rosa's eyes flickered to meet Joanne's. For a long moment the two girls stared at one another, and then Rosa's thick lashes fell, masking her expression. But that she now felt secure was revealed at once by her shocked exclamation.

'How dreadful! Don't you know who it was, Mrs. Barrie?'

Joanne's eyes opened wide. The swiftness with which the Portuguese girl had regained her composure, and the blatant hypocrisy of her question, almost took Joanne's breath away. She wished with all her heart she could reveal the truth, even at this late stage, but that was quite impossible. Instead she said, in quiet, yet quivering tones,

'No, Dona Rosa, I – I have no idea who the driver was.'

A deep sigh of relief? Perhaps . . . but after the first few seconds Dona Rosa had not really been afraid. Joanne had not given her away in the beginning, so she would be most unlikely to do so now.

'Where is your little girl?' asked Rosa curiously.

'At the farm.' Dom Manoel answered for Joanne, at the

same time leaning over to take the empty glass from her hand. 'I've arranged for her to be brought here; they'll stay the night. Doctor Mendes will be along directly to attend the child.'

The slow movement in Dona Rosa's throat revealed far more to Joanne than the Portuguese girl would have wished. She spoke at length, in slow and clearly protesting tones,

'Is this necessary, Manoel? Surely Mrs. Barrie would prefer to be at home, where she can care for her child in her own way?'

'Mrs. Barrie isn't in a fit condition to have full charge of her. She requires rest and quiet herself. Luisa will look to the child for tonight.'

Joanne glanced swiftly at him, noted the firm line of his jaw, and offered no objection to the arrangements he had made for her and Glee. In fact, she was having to admit that it was a relief to be managed in this way, to lean on someone else for a change, especially someone as coolly efficient as Dom Manoel. For a moment she pictured herself alone at the farm, trying to dress Glee's wounds, feeling sick with anxiety as to whether they were more serious than she imagined. It wasn't as if she had any near neighbours; the village was over half a mile away, down in the hollow between two low hills. She could never have reached it, for Glee couldn't have been left for more than a few minutes in case she came round in Joanne's absence.

Dom Manoel had taken the glass, and Joanne thanked him graciously, managing a rather wan little smile.

'It's most kind of you,' she offered with genuine sincerity. 'I'm afraid I've put you to a great deal of trouble – but I really didn't know where to turn. I'm very sorry for rushing into your house the way I did, but I was so afraid ...'

'Certainly you were afraid, which is natural. Forget all about it, Mrs. Barrie. It would seem to me that you've had quite enough anxiety and I want you to try and relax.' A frown darkened his brow and it was not difficult to guess at his thoughts. 'I expect you had to carry your little girl back to the house all by yourself?'

'Yes, I did.' Joanne looked up, and the expression she encountered in Rosa's eyes made her gasp. The girl actually hated her! But why? Bewildered, Joanne searched around for some valid reason, but before she could dwell for more than a few seconds on the question she heard voices in the hall and Dom Manoel instantly rose to his feet.

'Here they come, Mrs. Barrie – but stay where you are for a while. You can't do anything until the doctor arrives, so sit back and rest.'

He left the room. Rosa moved languidly to the chair he had vacated, and sat down.

'Why didn't you tell him the truth?' she asked, lifting one elegant hand to examine her finger nails. The action was calculated to give the impression of disinterest, but Joanne was not fooled.

'I would have told Dom Manoel,' she admitted, 'but I didn't think he'd believe me.'

'Wouldn't take your word against mine, you mean?'

'So you would have denied it?' came Joanne's swift rejoinder. 'I guessed as much.'

'Most certainly.' A pause and then, softly, 'And, Mrs. Barrie, if ever you change your mind and decide to tell him what really happened, I shall still deny it.'

'I see we understand one another.' Contempt for this girl rose like a suffocating cloak around Joanne. She wondered what kind of a wife she would make to Dom Manoel. Until now Joanne had believed them to be suited, but the happenings of the past few minutes had given her cause for doubt. The frigid and pompous exterior which Dom Manoel presented to the world was obviously misleading.

'Why didn't you wait for the doctor to come? I told you I'd ring him?'

'Did you ring him?' inquired Joanne, knowing full well that Dona Rosa had thought no more about the matter.

'I forgot, I must admit.'

'How very strange. Were I to knock a child down it would remain on my mind for a very long while.'

A sneer rose to the dark girl's lips.

'I'm being treated to another dose of your insolence, it seems.'

Joanne was saved from replying as, opening the door, Dom Manoel beckoned to her.

'The doctor's here. Your daughter's already in bed and Luisa will take you up. You may stay until the doctor goes and then you must get some rest yourself. Your room's ready and one of the maids will bring you up a sedative when you're in bed.'

Rising, Joanne caught Rosa's expression. She was staring at Dom Manoel, and appeared to be inwardly seething with anger. It was clear that she resented the attention Joanne was receiving from Dom Manoel. Was she regretting her refusal to take Glee to hospital? Joanne wondered, moving to the door. Had she done so then she, Joanne, would not be here, receiving hospitality from the man who had hitherto extended to her – at the best – a cool and rather bored civility.

'You're very kind,' Joanne was saying half an hour later when, to her utter astonishment, Dom Manoel himself appeared at her bedside with the sedative. 'Did the doctor speak to you about Glee?' She herself had questioned him, but all he said was that Glee needed care for a few weeks, adding that she had been very lucky indeed not to have sustained more serious injuries.

'Yes, Mrs. Barrie.' Dom Manoel spoke abruptly, in tones that caused Joanne to eye him with rising anxiety. 'Glee will need expert care for a long while, care which I'm quite sure you won't be able to afford.' He paused and Joanne frowned. Was he referring to the doctor's fees? He must be, and her heart gave a sudden jerk as she wondered where on earth she would find the money. 'Sit up and drink this—'

'But – Dom Manoel—'

'We'll discuss the matter in the morning,' he told her quietly. 'Now do as I say and drink this; it's to make you sleep.'

'I don't want to sleep,' she quivered, her voice edged with tears. 'I want to think!'

'And that's exactly what I intend to avoid.' He stood over her, waiting, and she sat up.

'If I could get home,' she began, when he interrupted with a sharp, exasperated sigh.

'Mrs. Barrie, why do you persist in trying my patience in this way? I've everything well in hand – and I do deplore fuss! Take this and let's have no more argument for the present.'

Her eyes met his; she expected to see the irritability of his voice reflected there, but he astonished her once again, this time by the sympathetic expression with which he regarded her.

'I'm sorry,' she whispered, adding, in a voice that was far from steady, 'It must be – nerves, I suppose.'

'Probably,' he quickly agreed. 'You've had a nasty shock, Mrs. Barrie, and that's why I'm determined you shall have a long and refreshing sleep.' She took the glass from him and swallowed the medicine. Dom Manoel watched her, nodding his approval when at last she handed him the empty glass. 'Lie down.' Joanne obeyed and he pulled up the covers on to her shoulders. 'You'll be asleep in a couple of minutes,' he said, and after regarding her inscrutably for a second or two he quietly left the room.

She watched him go, a strange wonderment stealing over her at the miraculous change in his whole demeanour in the face of her need – and her helplessness. He had not asked why she should have come to him; probably he took it for granted that, being her only near neighbour, he would naturally be the one to whom she would run for help. Little did he know that she had considered it his duty to help, seeing that it was his fiancée who was responsible for the plight in which Joanne had found herself.

Joanne's mind was becoming hazy, but through the mist she saw again Dom Manoel's expression as he stood beside Glee's bed. She had come round, had been made comfortable with her wounds speedily dressed and bandages applied where necessary. Still dazed, Glee had smiled wanly at everyone, including Dom Manoel, but his face was harsh in spite of the responding curve of his lips.

Still angry at the idea of anyone's knocking Glee down and then refusing to help, concluded Joanne, and wondered what he would say were he ever to discover the truth.

'I must stay with her,' Joanne had said urgently as Dom Manoel made to usher her from Glee's room. 'She can't possibly be left—'

'My dear Mrs. Barrie,' he put in with a sort of bored impatience, 'I'm well aware that she can't be left. Luisa will remain with her until two in the morning, and then she'll be relieved by Mafalda who, if my instructions have been carried out, is already taking a rest in preparation for *her* vigil.'

She should have known, thought Joanne, hovering now on the edge of sleep, she should have known that Dom Manoel would think of everything, down to the very last detail.

Turning, she found a cool part of the pillow and put her hot cheek against it and, as the last hazy thought drifted through her mind it was not of Glee or the accident, but of the attitude of Dom Manoel towards herself. How gently he had led her to the couch and sat her down; how quickly he had observed that she too was suffering from shock and needed a rest. And then, as if to strengthen the proof that he really was human, he had come to her room himself with the medicine. True, he had spoken sharply to her when she had talked of getting home, but then he had informed her that everything was well in hand ... well in hand ...? Joanne yawned into the pillow. What could he mean ...?

CHAPTER FOUR

JOANNE stood on the square, turreted tower, gazing dreamily out over the valley to the tiny village with its cluster of
stone houses lining the cobbled street. Although it was the
middle of November the air was pleasantly warm, and
smelled freshly of rain. From below she heard children's
laughter; Filipa and Leonor were playing in the old nursery,
the beautiful apartment which Dom Manoel had converted
into a schoolroom immediately on Joanne's taking up her
appointment as English instructress to his nieces.

A thoughtful frown creased her brow as she recalled the
way she had been 'blackmailed' into accepting the post. She
had tried to resist, but for some incomprehensible reason
Dom Manoel had been determined to make her succumb to
his wishes, and Joanne still did not know whether it was
because he could not bear to have his will opposed or
whether he had some reason of his own for wanting her to
stay at the Solar de Alvares. For he could so easily have
solved her problem by buying the farm and allowing her to
retain the tenancy until Glee was well again and fit to be
moved. Instead, he wasted no time in informing her of the
way in which he 'had everything well in hand'.

'Glee requires expert medical care, and this she'll receive
from my doctor. Were you to take her back to the farm she
couldn't possibly have this care – and in any case, it would
not be good for the child to be moved, even that short distance.' He had then offered her the post, emphasizing the
fact that she had no choice but to accept it.

'If you would buy my farm, Dom Manoel—?' But he
shook his head, reasserting his loss of interest in it. This
adamant attitude puzzled her extremely, for she felt sure he
still desired to incorporate the land into the Quinta de
Alvares. 'I'll sell it for the price of our fares home,' she
added impulsively, and Dom Manoel brought her up

sharply, causing her to blush at the foolishness of that remark.

'Don't you ever think before you speak? I've just said it will not be good for your daughter to be moved. You can't possibly be contemplating flying her home in this condition—? Or are you stubborn enough to go to those lengths?'

Joanne bit her lip, and lowered her head.

'No, Dom Manoel, I'm not thinking of flying Glee home yet awhile.'

'Then don't talk such nonsense about selling the farm so cheaply,' and he added on a distinct note of anger, 'Do you suppose I'd take it from you for such a small sum?'

Joanne spread her hands bewilderedly. Here was an inconsistency that she was quite unable to fathom.

'I can't find a buyer, Dom Manoel; you're fully aware of that.'

'Unfortunate,' he returned, apparently tired of the subject. 'Very unfortunate, Mrs. Barrie, but there it is. The place is in a most dilapidated state.' Dismissing the matter, he then went on to discuss the post he was offering to her. 'You'll be most comfortable here, with your own private suite. I'll pay you a good salary – but only on condition that you agree to stay until your services are no longer required – that is, until Filipa and Leonor can go back to their mother.'

'But I'm not qualified to teach English,' she protested, and to her surprise Dom Manoel merely shrugged his shoulders.

'You speak the language, so what more is necessary?'

Frowning in puzzlement, Joanne regarded him in silence. That Dom Manoel was determined to have his way there was no doubt, and Joanne finally capitulated, having no other choice, with Glee lying upstairs, bruised and grazed and suffering more badly from shock than was at first realized. She might just as well have agreed to Dom Manoel's proposal in the first place, thought Joanne, for now she came to consider it, she would have been most reluctant to move

Glee, even had Dom Manoel been more co-operative and bought the farm from her.

'And you'll promise to remain until the children go home to their mother?' he asked when she had agreed to take the post.

'Yes, I'll stay.'

He stared at her thoughtfully for a moment, and then,

'Obviously you'll soon save the fares which you require to take you back to England, but you've made a promise, and I believe you'll keep it.'

'Certainly I'll keep it,' came the indignant rejoinder. 'I don't make promises with the intention of breaking them!'

But little did she know of the difficulty she was to experience in keeping that promise.

A cool breeze came up, stirring the flag on the tower, and Joanne went down the steps into the house proper. Glee had been fast asleep when she had looked into her room a few minutes ago, but Joanne went past her sitting-room and along the corridor, with the intention of looking in on Glee again. To her surprise she heard voices and instinctively slackened her steps.

Rosa! What was she doing in Glee's room? The door was ajar; Joanne stood just outside and listened to the conversation.

'A long while ago – when you first came here – I asked if you knew what kind of a car it was that hit you, and you said you hadn't seen it. Can you think now what kind of a car it was?'

Joanne stiffened. Glee had not mentioned anything about being questioned – but from Rosa's words it would appear she had put the question at a time when Glee was very poorly indeed.

'No, because I just ran to the side when I heard it. I think ... I think it was a blue one— No, it was a green one ... I think ...'

'You don't really know, do you, dear?' Rosa's voice was

60

soft, almost gentle. Joanne felt suffocated with disgust.

'No, Dona Rosa, I don't really know.'

'If someone said it was a black one, you'd definitely say it wasn't?'

'It might have been a black one—'

'No, Glee, it wasn't a black one. You've just said it might have been a blue one. Well, it was a blue one.'

'Was it, Dona Rosa? How do you know? Did you see it?'

A smile curved Joanne's lips. Dona Rosa had underestimated Glee's intelligence. Joanne just had to walk in, for she was most curious to see Rosa's reaction to Glee's rather clever response to her statement.

'Well, Dona Rosa, did you see it?' Joanne said when the other girl merely stood there, staring at Glee.

Rosa flushed, but it did not take her long to recover her self-possession.

'No, I didn't see it, Mrs. Barrie, but there are several blue cars about and I thought it might be one of those.'

'You're speaking for Glee's benefit, I take it?' murmured Joanne, almost inaudibly.

'Well, certainly not for yours,' came the challenging retort, and, after a small pause, 'Remember what I said, Mrs. Barrie. If ever you should change your mind . . .'

'You'll deny it all.'

'Exactly . . . and as you yourself deduced, my word would be stronger than yours.'

'I haven't the slightest doubt it would carry more weight, Dona Rosa, and for that reason you're quite safe.' And, her eyes roving over her in a swift, contemptuous glance, Joanne brushed past the Portuguese girl and moved across the room to the bed. 'If you've quite finished questioning Glee, perhaps you'll leave us,' she said over her shoulder, and a sound like a hiss came from between Rosa's even white teeth.

'Your manners don't appear to have improved with your environment,' she said with a sneer.

'Unfortunately they're affected by the company I'm compelled to keep.' Joanne busied herself with smoothing the pillows behind Glee's back. Had she turned, however, she would have surprised a look of such intense hatred that she might have regretted her swift retaliation to Dona Rosa's disparaging comment on her manners.

The following afternoon Joanne was in the schoolroom when Dom Manoel came in with a book which he offered to lend her.

'You mentioned that you'd half read it in England, and then had to leave it when you came out here. I had an idea it was in my library – and in English – so I made an effort and found it for you.'

'You're very kind.' His action surprised her, for she had merely mentioned the matter in passing, one day when they happened to be discussing books. 'What really happened was that the book belonged to my brother, and although I would have liked to finish it, I felt I should return it to him.'

'You have a brother, then?' Joanne nodded and he smiled. 'Perhaps he'll come over and visit you sometime. I'm sure you'd like a visit from him?'

'Yes, I would,' she returned, because that was the answer Dom Manoel expected of her, but Joanne reflected for a space on the complications which would arise were she to have a visit from Roger. On first hearing of the accident he had expressed a desire to come over, but as he had not mentioned it in his last letter, he had been prevented either by lack of money or by his wife who, right from the first, had exerted far too much influence over him. But Joanne had mixed feelings about his failure to come, for on his arrival Glee would instantly have referred to him as daddy and this would naturally have necessitated explanations to Dom Manoel.

Recently, Joanne had begun to feel she had risen in Dom Manoel's estimation, and she rather thought he would be more than a little disgusted on hearing of her deception, and for some reason she could not explain she hated the idea of his discovering she was living a lie, as it were. It had all been so unnecessary, resulting purely from that stubborn streak in her nature. As Chris had said at the time, she, Joanne, should have corrected Dom Manoel's mistake immediately it had been made, but had been so irritated by his pompous and disagreeable manner that she had been too impatient and disinterested to explain. If he liked to jump to conclusions why should she take the trouble to disillusion him? As she had remarked to Chris, their paths would never cross again, so what did it matter? Little did she guess then what was to transpire! And Joanne now heartily wished she had put him in possession of the facts in the first place.

'Is your brother married?' inquired Dom Manoel, breaking into her thoughts.

'Yes.' She felt uncomfortable – had felt like this in his presence for the past week. 'It's very good of you to fetch the book,' she added, simply for something to say.

'I was coming in, in any case.' He moved over to see what the children were doing. 'I felt it was time I took some interest in their progress.'

'Don't they go to school?' Joanne asked curiously, and Dom Manoel shook his head.

'They had a governess until about a month ago, but she left to get married. It's not worth replacing her now, for the children will be going home immediately after Christmas – at least I think they will. I'm hoping my sister will be out of hospital then.'

'I'm doing very well, Uncle Manoel,' interposed Filipa, lifting her head to look at him adoringly. This affection between the children and their uncle had come as a complete shock to Joanne, for somehow she had gained the impression that his outward cold austerity would be extended to all around him. But to her utter astonishment she had actually surprised him with both children on his knees, his arms around them, looking at a book they were showing to him. She had come down from her own sitting-room to inquire about some exercise paper and notebooks which Dom Manoel had promised to get for her, and she stopped in the doorway, so great was her surprise at the intimate little scene before her.

Dom Manoel had looked up ... and then it was that Joanne had seen him with a softened expression, the expression that she had known would transform him into the most outstandingly attractive man she had ever encountered. And from that moment on she had experienced this peculiar discomfort when in his presence.

'Senhora Barrie is much pleased with me.'

'Is she, Filipa? I'm glad to hear it.' He glanced over to Joanne; for no apparent reason a rosy flush spread over her face, highlighting the delicate contours of her cheeks and brow. Her awkwardness increased; she had the extraordinary impulse to stand, merely because she was in his presence. The idea brought an involuntary quiver to her lips, and a curious light entered Dom Manoel's eyes. It was some time before he withdrew his gaze and returned his attention to what his niece was writing.

'I had all my lessons right yesterday,' submitted Leonor, not to be outdone by her sister. 'And Senhora Barrie said I have the cleverness.' She looked uncertainly at him, aware of saying something which was not quite correct. Her uncle's brows rose in a gesture of admonishment, but Leonor only grinned. 'I am – I am much clever! There, that is better!'

'A little,' he conceded, then told them both to get on with their work. 'I've been thinking,' he said to Joanne, returning to the desk at which she sat. 'As you know, Leonor has a birthday party on Sunday, and I don't see why Glee can't come downstairs – after all, she's been getting up a little for the past few days. She's a splendid little patient and I think he deserves the change.' He stopped, looking at the marking upon which Joanne had been engaged when he interrupted her. 'What's this?'

'The work they did before lunch.'

'But how long are you working?'

'Four hours a day.'

'I told you to work two,' he returned sharply.

'Yes, but – well, I wasn't earning my money—'

'That's a question for me to decide. You can't leave Glee

64

for four hours a day!'

'Luisa stays with her when I'm not there – or Mafalda—' She turned in her chair, adding impulsively, but in lowered tones so as not to be overheard by the children, 'Dom Manoel, you're doing far too much for me. I really don't understand why you should.'

From outside came the loud and grating noise made by the peacocks perched high in the trees, and Dom Manoel waited until all was quiet again before he spoke.

'I believe we're related, Mrs. Barrie.'

Her eyes widened.

'I surmised that you'd forgotten that.'

'Did you? Why?'

Joanne became flustered, not merely by the question but also by the rather quizzical lift of his brows. She searched for some words of explanation, but as nothing better presented itself she told him the truth.

'The difference in our positions, Dom Manoel. I took it for granted you wouldn't like the idea of our being related.' Not at all diplomatic, she realized – but only when it was too late.

Sudden anger took the place of the smile in his eyes.

'I don't remember having given you cause to consider me a snob,' he said stiffly, preparing to rise from his chair.

'I'm sorry.' Joanne spoke with haste; subconsciously she had a desire for him to remain and to her relief he leant back in his chair, relaxed. Changing the subject, he told her that although she was employed by him her first duty was to Glee.

'Luisa and Mafalda appear to have acquired a great affection for her – and she for them,' he continued, astonishing Joanne by his knowledge of what went on. 'But naturally it's her mother she wants. If you devote two hours daily to Filipa and Leonor I shall be quite satisfied.'

It just didn't make sense, reflected Joanne, shaking her head in a gesture of bewilderment.

'I'm not earning my money as it is. Also, the doctor's bills – I should be paying those, not you.'

'Doctor Mendes attends my nieces – and anyone else in the house who happens to need him. A little extra on his bill is nothing.' Passing that off as unimportant, he went on to inform Joanne that he had dismissed her man.

'The animals, and the fowls—' she began, imagining them to be starving.

'One of my men is going over each day at present, but I suggest you sell the livestock; it isn't as if it's making you any profit at all.'

Joanne moved uncomfortably. It wasn't easy for her to admit that Dom Manoel had been so right, and she herself so wrong.

'Who'll want to buy it?' she queried at last.

'I'll take it,' he offered after a small hesitation, and Joanne was compelled to say she was quite sure her animals weren't up to the standard of his own stock, and they must in any case be a loss to him. He made no remark on that and she went on,

'Luis? I owe him some money.'

'He's been paid all he's going to have.'

'You've paid him—? Oh, but this is wrong!' She shook her head again, her bewilderment increasing. 'I don't know why you're doing all this?' He must be aware of her puzzlement, yet he appeared to be idly listening to the peacocks who were uttering their raucous sounds again. 'I feel I haven't thanked you enough, Dom Manoel, but I really am grateful.'

He turned at that, and contemplated her in silence for a while, his whole demeanour one of uncertainty. Uncertainty? She must be imagining things, concluded Joanne, for the self-assured Dom Manoel Alvares would never find himself in an attitude of indecision.

'In that case,' he said at length, 'you'll probably be willing to do something for me in return?'

'Most certainly,' she agreed without stopping to consider what a man like Dom Manoel could possibly want of her. 'I'll do anything.'

'Anything?' His lips actually quivered in amusement, and Joanne felt a little rush of colour to her cheeks.

'I'm sure you wouldn't ask anything too difficult of me, Dom Manoel.'

'No, Mrs. Barrie, you're quite right, I wouldn't.' A pause, and then, 'So you're quite prepared to do some little thing for me?'

'Quite,' she returned after only the merest hesitation, and then, on a note of sudden shyness, 'What is it you want me to do?'

'For the present, nothing. I'll tell you about it when I'm ready.'

The children were having a wonderful time; the room where they had their tea had been beautifully decorated with flowers and lights and brilliantly coloured streamers. The room in which the games were being held had also been decorated especially for the occasion, and the carpets had been taken up so that the children could dance. A group of musicians arrived to play for them; they were attractively clad in their native costumes and added enormously to the gaiety with the playing of the pipes and the mandolins and guitars.

Dom Manoel's mother and stepfather were there and Joanne met them for the first time.

Despite the smallness of her stature Dona Clementina was a proud and arrogant woman, distinguished and highly intelligent, with scarcely a wrinkle on her dark handsome face. Her husband on the other hand was far more amiable, and Joanne found herself thoroughly enjoying his company when, during the games, he invited her to sit down beside him on the sofa. His wife sat on the other side of the room with her son, but Joanne felt her eyes on her the whole time . . . eyes that were far from friendly.

'Tell me how you come to be here?' Senhor Pedro de Castro's eyes flickered over her appreciatively as Joanne smilingly occupied the seat next to him. 'Your presence here came as a complete surprise, for my stepson had not previously mentioned you. You're a widow, he now informs us.'

67

Ignoring that last remark, Joanne explained all that had happened, keeping back only the fact of Dona Rosa's having been responsible for the accident to Glee. She had also kept it from Ricardo, for she knew he would tell his mother who, Joanne suspected, would gossip in the village and the information could eventually come to Dom Manoel's ears. As far as Joanne was concerned the matter was finished with; she would never deliberately cause dissension between Dom Manoel and his fiancée.

'You came here to farm Pendela all on your own?' His dark eyes widened with admiration. 'You're a very brave girl.'

But Joanne shook her head rather sadly.

'A foolish one, as it's turned out,' she responded wryly. 'Dom Manoel was right when he said I'd never make it pay.'

'But you'll sell it to him now?'

'He doesn't want it.'

Senhor de Castro evinced some considerable surprise.

'He's told you this?'

'Dom Manoel has refused to buy the farm, yes.'

He lifted a chubby brown hand and stroked his chin thoughtfully.

'How very odd. Manoel has always wanted the place – has, I believe, actually resented the fact of its being separated from the estate in the first place. You see, with all due respect to you, my dear, it is a bit of an eyesore, as it's been neglected for many years. It mars the view from the front of his house.'

'I should have accepted his offer in the first place,' she sighed. 'It's my own fault if I've lost everything.'

Senhor de Castro continued to stroke his chin, a reflective expression on his round, good-humoured face.

'There must be some good reason for his attitude ... I wonder what it can be?' Following the direction of his gaze Joanne saw that Dom Manoel and his mother were deep in conversation. Dona Clementina glanced across at Joanne, then said something to her son. Joanne experienced an odd

68

feeling of discomfort, for she felt certain she was being discussed. Dona Clementina cast another glance in Joanne's direction, a glance of thinly-veiled hostility and a frown creased Senhor de Castro's forehead. 'Yes, there's a reason,' he murmured softly. 'I wonder what it can be?'

A few minutes later Dom Manoel disappeared and his mother came over to join her husband and Joanne.

'What are you two talking about?' she wanted to know, adding, 'It could almost be a conspiracy, judging by your expression, Pedro.' The arrogant voice jarred, and Joanne searched for some excuse to leave this woman's company. However, to do so immediately would be ill-mannered, and she answered her question instead.

'I was telling Senhor de Castro how I came to be here.'

'My son was telling me the same thing.' From her seat opposite Dona Clementina looked at Joanne up and down, taking in every detail of her appearance. 'Why Manoel should want an English instructress for Leonor and Filipa is quite beyond me. He's never troubled his head about their English before. If their mother had considered it necessary she'd have seen to the matter before now.'

Her forthright declaration amounted almost to rudeness and two bright spots of colour sprang to Joanne's cheeks. A fitting mother-in-law for Dona Rosa, she decided, curbing the angry retort that rose to her lips.

'I expect your son knows what he's doing,' she quietly returned.

'I expect he does. . . .' It was Senhor de Castro who spoke, and there was a most odd inflection in his voice. He glanced round the room. 'Where is Rosa? I haven't seen her since tea time.' The adults had taken their tea in the salon, away from the children; all except Rosa had then joined the party, although Joanne strongly suspected an occasion such as this was not exactly to Dona Clementina's taste. 'She should be here, with the children.'

'If Rosa wishes to escape from such a gathering then it's her own affair. You speak as if it's a duty she should perform.'

Senhor de Castro's good humour remained, in spite of his wife's tart response to his comment.

'It would be a duty only if she were going to be married to Manoel,' came the mild observation. 'If, on the other hand, they are not to be married—'

'Certainly they're to be married,' his wife haughtily interrupted. 'Everyone expects it.'

He smiled benignly at her. 'Things don't always turn out as people expect. For myself, I've never considered Rosa a good match for your son.'

'She has wealth, and the connections necessary for the position of mistress here at the Solar de Alvares. I should be greatly disappointed if Manoel did not marry her.'

A long pause; feeling extremely uncomfortable Joanne rose from the couch. She was about to make her excuses when Senhor de Castro spoke in his soft and pleasant tones.

'It could be that Manoel will surprise us all by marrying for love.'

'He loves Rosa,' snapped his wife, and Senhor de Castro's eyes opened very wide.

'My dear, no one could love Rosa—'

'If you'll excuse me,' interrupted Joanne hastily, 'I must go and see how Glee is. She'll probably be very tired by this time.

She had noticed that Glee was not dancing, and found her at the far end of the room, sitting on a couch. Dom Manoel stood in the great carved doorway, surveying the gay scene before him when, having spotted Glee, he made his way towards her, reaching her side at the same time as Joanne.

'How is our little invalid enjoying herself.' Looking thoroughly human in light grey slacks and a loose-fitting jacket, with a bright green party hat perched at an angle on his head, Dom Manoel sat down on the couch and took Glee's small hand in his. 'Are you tired?'

Glee shook her head vigorously, and as Joanne and Dom Manoel caught each other's glance they both smiled. Glee would never give in, they were thinking, but both were also wondering if the excitement was becoming too much for her.

'I'm not a little bit tired,' Glee declared, smiling at Dom Manoel. Somehow, thought Joanne, he had managed to dispel the first unfavourable impression he made on the child. 'It's fun. I've never been to a party like this before.' Some of the servants had been standing around, and now one or two of them joined in the dancing. Glee clapped her hands excitedly. 'Mummy, why don't you dance?'

'I don't know how to do it, Glee.' She turned her head, moved by some odd force. Dona Rosa was standing by the door, having just entered the room. The look of boredom on her face was unmistakable, but a smile broke as her eyes lighted on Dom Manoel. With easy languid steps she moved between the dancers, reaching him just as he rose to his feet and held out a hand to Joanne. Obviously he had not seen Rosa, concluded Joanne, for he never even turned as she came up to him.

'Come, Joanne, Glee wants to see you dancing.'

Joanne. . . . She gaped at him, but he seemed quite indifferent to her confusion as, pulling her to her feet, he urged her towards the circle of dancers.

'I c-can't do it,' she stammered, her eyes meeting those of Rosa, who was staring at her in furious disbelief.

'You'll soon learn the steps,' he assured her. 'There's nothing to them.'

'But – really—' She was swept away, into the circle, stumbling at first but soon falling into step. Everyone was delighted with the idea of Dom Manoel's joining in the dance, and despite the chaos of her mind Joanne found to her surprise that she was actually enjoying herself. Dom Manoel was in the ring next to her, holding one of her hands. She felt the warmth of his touch, sensed the hidden strength beneath the light and careless clasp of his fingers, and a most odd sensation entered into her. Never had she expected to be disturbed in this way by the man who, on their first meeting, had managed to instil into her a dislike so intense

71

that she believed it would remain with her for ever.

'You see, it's quite simple.' He smiled at her as they danced; then the music stopped and they returned to the couch. Dona Rosa was sitting on a chair, trying to talk to Glee, but Glee was too interested in watching Joanne, and she laughed delightedly as Joanne sat down next to her, panting a little from her exertions.

'You did it very good, Mummy, but Dom Manoel helped you, didn't he?'

'Nothing of the kind. Your mummy learnt all by herself.'

'I saw you helping her.' Glee looked at him accusingly. 'You put your foot out, sideways, and told Mummy to do the same.'

'Perhaps you're right.' He stood by the couch, his dark eyes travelling from Glee to Joanne and back again. 'How alike you are,' he murmured, almost to himself. Joanne blushed, feeling ashamed of her deceit and wondering what Dom Manoel would say were he ever to make the discovery that Glee was not her daughter.

Dona Rosa was also looking from one to the other, an ugly line curving her mouth; and then her gaze wandered to Joanne's hand and her attention became fixed on the wedding ring she wore. What was she thinking? Joanne frowned suddenly and a prickly feeling passed along her spine. It was ridiculous, but she felt a fear of this girl, had the firm conviction that she would harm her if she could.

The music started up again, and Dona Rosa transferred her gaze to Dom Manoel, clearly inviting him to dance with her, even though she still appeared to be bored with the whole affair. Whether or not Dom Manoel would have complied with the unspoken request Joanne never knew, for Glee chose that moment to yawn, and Dom Manoel gave a firm and decisive nod of his head.

'Right, young lady. Upstairs you go.'

'Oh, but I'm not tired.' Protestingly she looked at him. Glee was no respecter of positions, and although Dom Manoel was looking rather sternly at her she went on to add,

'I want to stay till the end.'

'You're going to bed now.'

Glee shook her head and leant back against the cushions, watching the dancers.

'What an undisciplined child!' exclaimed Rosa, glancing at her with acute dislike. 'Does Glee always argue in this way, Mrs. Barrie?'

Joanne coloured. It was not like Glee to be disobedient, but Joanne could understand her reluctance to leave when the other children were enjoying themselves.

'You're not used to children, Dona Rosa,' she said, speaking her thoughts aloud. 'It's natural that Glee should want to stay.'

'Natural that she should defy authority.' She shrugged. 'It's not that I don't understand children, Mrs. Barrie. It's the method by which you're bringing your child up that I fail to understand.'

Too impatient to comment on that, Joanne gave her attention to Glee.

'Come, darling, you must do as Dom Manoel says.' She caught his expression as he glanced at Rosa. His eyes were hard and arrogant, his jaw flexed.

Glee made to get off the couch, but changed her mind and looked coaxingly up at Dom Manoel.

'Please can I stay for a little while longer?' Her thick dark lashes fluttered; she would know just how to manage the men when she grew older, her grandmother had once said, and to Joanne's amazement she now appeared to be affecting Dom Manoel in some strange way, for his whole demeanour changed and he actually smiled as he said,

'Ten minutes, then – and only ten minutes, because you're already nearly asleep.'

A gasp escaped Rosa, and an unfathomable light entered her eyes. Presently she looked at Dom Manoel, again inviting him to dance, but the music stopped and everyone sat down while sweets were handed round to the children. Glee tried valiantly to keep awake, but even before the ten minutes had elapsed she was dozing against the cushions.

Dom Manoel rose and picked her up. She opened her eyes, then nestled her head against his shoulder.

'My present, Mummy, it's behind the cushion.' She stretched out an arm.

Each child had received a gift, and Glee's was a charming little handbag in bright red leather. Taking it from behind the cushion, Joanne handed it to her.

'Manoel . . . surely you're not carrying the child up yourself?' The question came sharply from Rosa, who was clearly seething by this time. In all fairness Joanne had to sympathize with her, for Dom Manoel had not so much as spoken to her from the moment she joined them. And he should have danced with her, thought Joanne, wondering if they'd had a quarrel.

'Does she look able to walk up?' he inquired, and Joanne caught her breath at the sudden arrogance in his voice. They must have quarrelled, she concluded, and much as she disliked the girl she felt a certain disappointment at the way in which Dom Manoel treated her. He was punishing her for something, and the method he adopted caused him to fall in Joanne's estimation. Such petty spite denoted a weakness which was totally out of character.

Blushing angrily, Rosa stiffened and fell silent.

'Say good night.' Dom Manoel nodded to Diego and the old man held up a hand for silence. 'Glee is tired, children, and wants to bid you good night.' Dom Manoel then repeated that in his own language; the rather blank expressions disappeared from the faces of the children and bright spontaneous smiles were cast in Glee's direction.

While Glee sleepily said her good nights Joanne's eyes wandered to Rosa. Her face was a study as she watched Dom Manoel with Glee in his arms. No doubt about it, mused Joanne, Rosa was bitterly regretting her refusal to take her to the hospital. Little had she guessed, on leaving Joanne there in the middle of the road, with the senseless child in her arms, just what the outcome of her heartless action would be.

Upstairs, in Glee's room, Dom Manoel laid Glee carefully down on the bed. She opened her eyes, her tiredness leaving her for a moment.

'Thank you for letting me go to the party,' she said.

'You enjoyed yourself?'

'Yes; it was lovely.'

'The next time you'll be able to join in everything, for very soon you're going to be quite well again.'

Startled, Joanne reminded Dom Manoel that they wouldn't be here for the next party, as Filipa's birthday was not until October of the following year.

'You'll be here for Christmas,' he said, throwing her a questioning look.

'Of course, I forgot about Christmas.'

Christmas in a Portuguese great house really was something, Ricardo had told her, though at the time Joanne had not the remotest idea of ever partaking in such festivities.

Glee's eyelids drooped and Dom Manoel advised Joanne to undress her while she was still awake.

'Yes, I will.' Awkwardness swept over her as she added, 'Good night, Dom Manoel, and thank you for being so good to Glee.'

'Don't thank me, Joanne. As I've said, I shall be requiring something in return.'

She glanced swiftly at him. Somehow she felt there was a connection between his referring to her as Joanne, and whatever it was he desired of her. Although aware of her curiosity he proffered no explanation, and the matter continued to puzzle her so much that she found herself mentioning it to Ricardo the next time she saw him. She had gone into the village and unexpectedly come across him in one of the shops.

'Joanne! I thought you'd fallen out with me. I haven't seen you for a week.'

'Is it a week?' she asked unbelievingly. Time had never passed so quickly as it had since she and Glee had taken up their residence at the Solar de Alvares almost a month ago. 'Is it really a week since I called to see your mother?'

'I flattered myself that it was me you came to see,' he said teasingly.

'I came to see you both.'

'You mean that?'

'I mean it,' she replied seriously, and impulsively he took her arm.

'Come and have a coffee,' he invited, relieving her of her shopping bag. 'I had begun to wonder whether I dared ring you up. Would it have been all right?'

'I should think so. Dom Manoel wouldn't have minded, I'm sure.'

'You appear to have softened him up,' he declared with a grimace, and it was then that Joanne told Ricardo about Dom Manoel's strange request that she should do something for him. 'And you've no idea what it is?' he asked, puzzled.

Joanne shook her head.

'He seems most reluctant to tell me.'

'He's waiting for something, you mean?'

'I don't know. It's all so mystifying. If he wants me to do something for him why can't he tell me now?'

Ricardo thought about it for a moment and then shrugged his shoulders.

'It can't be anything important, Joanne. Forget it; he'll tell you when he's ready.' They had reached the café, and a few minutes later they were drinking their coffee and Ricardo was inquiring about Glee.

'She's progressing very well – though the effect on her nervous system was far worse than we'd imagined. She gets up now, and last Sunday she went downstairs to Leonor's party.'

'Dom Manoel let her?' His swift glance of surprise brought to Joanne's mind her own previous conclusion that Dom Manoel was an arrant snob.

'He actually carried her up to her room when she became tired.'

'He did—? What have you done to him!'

'I haven't done anything,' she laughed. 'It just happens

that he's not nearly so formidable as he appears.

'But you've only to *look* at him!'

'I admit he does seem rather awe-inspiring when you don't know him.'

'But improves on acquaintance, I gather?'

Most certainly Dom Manoel had improved on acquaintance, she mused, reflecting on his swift response to her plea for help and, later, his gentleness with Glee.

Their coffee finished, Joanne and Ricardo stood for a while outside the café, chatting, while to and fro passed the native women, carrying great loads on their heads.

'How do they balance them?' Joanne wanted to know, fascinated at the ease and grace with which the women performed what to her seemed an impossible feat.

'They learn from being very young. The modern girls can't do it.'

'No?'

'They haven't had the practice.' A cart drawn by oxen came rumbling along the cobbled street, and the driver raised a hand in salute. 'The people here are very friendly, yes?'

'Very,' she answered, thinking of the way both Dom Manoel and his fiancée had given her a totally wrong first impression.

'You'd like to live here always?'

'It isn't possible, Ricardo.' She saw his changing expression, noting the frown appearing on his brow.

'You'll be staying for a while, though?'

'I've promised to remain while ever Dom Manoel needs me,' she reminded him. 'I don't know how long that will be.'

'You like me, Joanne?' he queried after a pause.

Joanne turned, holding out her hand for the basket he still carried. She liked Ricardo, but in what way she did not know herself. That he was attractive there was no doubt, and that he could care for her there was no doubt either. His mother, too, welcomed her in a way which suggested she would encourage a friendship between them. A little while ago Joanne had wondered if her feelings for Ricardo were the beginnings of love ... but now, for some reason she could not explain, she knew those feelings would never develop into anything stronger than friendship. Ricardo handed her the basket, his manner still one of inquiry.

'I like you, Ricardo, yes,' she murmured uneasily, and then, with some haste, 'I must be going. I've left Luisa with Glee, and I promised her I'd be back within the hour.'

'When shall I see you again?'

'It's awkward. I have my work, and also I don't like to leave Glee too often.'

'I'll ring you, then?' he said and she nodded. 'You never came to that meal,' he went on. 'Promise you'll come as soon as Glee is about again. Mother's been looking forward to it.'

'I'll come,' she smiled. 'But it won't be for at least a week.'

'As long as I know you're coming I'll be patient. When shall I ring you?'

'Any time — it doesn't matter. I'm always in.' And after saying good-bye she hurried away, wondering if she had been wise in making that promise. Ricardo was serious, she knew, while she herself experienced a confusion of mind for which there was no apparent explanation.

CHAPTER FIVE

NOVEMBER came to an end, and with it much of the activity of the wine-making. After the harvesting came the treading and sieving, then the addition of the chemicals necessary for fermentation. The wine was left for three or four weeks before being put into barrels and taken down the river to the wine cellars at Vila Nova de Gaia where it would be stored for several months before being sold. During all this activity there was much song and dance among the peasants engaged in the processing of the wine. Those people who came from a distance had their tents pitched on the *quinta* and every evening they would dance round their camp fires and the sounds of music and singing could be heard floating across the valley.

'You miss it when it's all over.' Joanne was sitting on the verandah, looking down to the hillside terraces which had recently produced such an abundance of grapes. Dom Manoel had joined her and they had been chatting for some time before Joanne made her remark about the festivities. Her voice held a tinge of regret and Dom Manoel regarded her in some amusement on hearing it.

'There's always another season,' he observed in softer and more friendly tones than she had ever before heard him use.

'I shan't be here this time next year.'

Dom Manoel flicked an imaginary speck of dust from his sleeve; Joanne was struck by the idea that he was carefully choosing his words.

'One can never say, Joanne, where one will be a year hence.'

'I can be sure I won't be in Portugal.' There was a sort of intimacy about him which embarrassed her and she glanced away, over to where the sun spread a veil of burnished tulle across the sky. As the great fiery ball disappeared below the earth's dark edge the crimson changed almost imperceptibly into an admixture of amethyst and pearl, and finally a deep purple mantle descended on the valley and hills and the distant forests of pine. The west wind, merely a zephyr, blew warm and fresh on her face, and stirred her hair into attractive disorder. Conscious of Dom Manoel's rather intense regard, she dwelt for a moment on the change that had taken place in their relationship since the evening of Leonor's party. Although he remained cool, retaining the impersonal manner of the employer, he had at the same time discarded that haughty air of superiority which had so irritated Joanne on their first and subsequent meetings. The change was naturally perceived by Dona Rosa, and when, just over a week ago, Dom Manoel had told Joanne it was not necessary for her and Glee to keep to their own rooms, but that they must in future treat the house as their home, Dona Rosa had made no effort to conceal her anger.

'You can't have other people's children running all over the place,' she protested, ignoring the steely glint that had entered Dom Manoel's dark eyes. 'I'm sure, in any case, that Mrs. Barrie would prefer to keep to her own apartments.'

What Dom Manoel said to that Joanne had never discovered, for he made a polite request that she should leave the room, and Joanne instantly complied, with genuine relief.

'How can you be so sure you won't be in Portugal?' he asked, interrupting Joanne's thoughts.

She looked at him rather wanly.

'I haven't the means to stay here, Dom Manoel,' she reminded him 'I lost everything on the farm.'

The admission, which would never have been made a few months ago, surprised Joanne as much as it surprised Dom Manoel. However, he made no comment on it and they fell once more into casual conversation until, complete darkness having fallen, Joanne said she must go indoors and see to Glee's supper.

'It's already past her bedtime,' she added, preparing to rise.

'I've told Mafalda to give Glee her supper and put her to bed,' he coolly informed her, and Joanne's eyes flew to his, for a most odd inflection had now entered his deep attractive voice.

'But I don't understand? I always see to Glee myself.'

'I've something important to say to you, Joanne.'

Having half risen from her chair, Joanne promptly sat down again, her pulses quickening. Instinctively she knew the time had come for her to honour the promise she had so eagerly made.

'What is it?' she asked breathlessly.

'I want you to become engaged to me.' So soft and unemotional a tone!

For one incredulous moment she could only sit there peering through the darkness, trying to examine his features and telling herself she had not heard aright. But the memory of several incidents, so puzzling at the time, now gave strength to the notion that Dom Manoel was in fact quite serious. His refusal to buy her farm – she now saw that as a deliberate move to force her into accepting a post in his house; the more accessible manner he had assumed, developing gradually into friendliness towards her; the dropping of the formality of addressing her as Mrs. Barrie. But there had never been a word or glance of affection.

'Dom Manoel,' she said in almost inaudible tones, 'you can't want to marry me.' What could have occurred between him and Dona Rosa? she wondered. Had they quarrelled again? – and was this some sort of revenge?

'I haven't said anything about marriage,' he smoothly corrected. 'I merely expressed a desire to become engaged to you.'

'You mean—?' She stopped, waiting in stupefied silence for him to continue, but he offered no explanation and she managed to finish, 'It's to be a temporary arrangement?'

'Exactly.'

'But why?'

'Naturally I've a good reason,' he remarked, stifling a yawn, 'but it need not concern you.'

The coolness of him! Did he think she would agree to his request, just like that?

'You want me to become engaged to you, without knowing why?' she gasped.

'You declared a willingness to do something for me,' he reminded her softly. 'I expect you to keep to your word.'

Joanne shook her head in blank bewilderment, and spoke her thoughts aloud.

'What about Dona Rosa?'

'Dona Rosa?' He reached up, to snap on the light. 'What has Dona Rosa to do with it?' he asked, eyeing her curiously.

'You and she are not engaged?'

No mistaking his surprise . . . and distaste. It would seem he actually disliked the girl.

'What gave you that idea?' he almost snapped.

The information had come from Luis, she recalled – and Luis had proved to be most unreliable in every way. Plainly the rumour had no foundation, and Joanne wondered at the feeling of relief sweeping over her at the knowledge.

Dom Manoel moved impatiently and, reluctant to admit having listened to the gossip of her farm hand, Joanne murmured rather feebly,

'I just concluded that you and Dona Rosa were engaged.'

He raised his dark brows unbelievingly.

'I can't think how you reached a conclusion like that. Were we engaged Dona Rosa would obviously be wearing my ring.'

'Yes, I realize that now.' She thought of his mother, confidently declaring her son to be in love with Rosa – and her husband's response that no one could love her. Joanne herself would not have been as definite as that, but with her new evaluation of Dom Manoel's character she had a growing conviction that he and his cousin were totally unsuited. It was an odd circumstance that, having initially disliked Dom Manoel intensely, declaring him to be a pompous, conceited snob, she now knew without any doubt at all that he was far too good for the arrogant and conscienceless Dona Rosa Fernandes.

Joanne looked across at Dom Manoel, wondering if he were aware of his mother's hopes regarding a marriage between him and Rosa. But it would not concern him, for always he would do as he pleased, never allowing anyone to influence his actions. He was now waiting in an attitude of bored impatience for her to add to her comment, but she allowed the subject of Rosa to drop.

'I can't become engaged to you without knowing the reason,' she ventured persuasively. 'Surely you can tell me a little more?'

'So you're breaking your promise,' he accused, ignoring her plea.

'I don't know what to say. It's so unexpected.'

'I'm not asking the impossible,' he pointed out with some asperity. 'You merely have to wear my ring for a few months. This is not going to cause you any inconvenience that I can see.'

True ... but Joanne considered his request unfair, and she told him so.

'I should at least know why I'm doing this,' she added reasonably.

But his inexorable expression was sufficient to convince Joanne that he had no intention of confiding in her. Either she must accede unconditionally to his wish, or she must break her promise. She hadn't any choice, for there existed no reasonable excuse for breaking her promise. As Dom Manoel said, he did not ask the impossible. How would Dona Rosa take it? she wondered, for it was abundantly clear that Rosa cherished hopes of becoming Dom Manoel's wife.

'I hope you'll endeavour to act as if you – care for me,' he requested when at length she consented to do as he wished. 'It will appear most odd if, for instance, you continue to address me as Dom Manoel.'

Odd to whom? There was only Rosa that Joanne could see. Was he doing this wholly for Rosa's benefit? – because he wanted to throw off the net which threatened to drag him into marriage? But no, that couldn't be, for Dom Manoel was not the man to resort to stratagem as a way out of the difficulty. He would be quite honest with Rosa regarding his feelings for her.

A soft flush had risen to Joanne's cheeks at Dom Manoel's words; he noticed it, with growing amusement, and as another thought suddenly struck her she thankfully changed the subject.

'When you saw me in England you offered me the post here – had you the engagement in mind then?'

'No.'

'Then why did you offer me the post?'

'As an inducement for you to give up the idea of farming Pendela and sell out to me. You mentioned you'd no other means of making a living, so I was merely providing you with one.'

'But later, when I wanted to sell you the farm. . . . ?'

'I refused.' He smiled quizzically at her. 'By that time I did have the engagement in mind.'

'It wasn't very kind to refuse me,' she said accusingly, 'when I was so desperate.'

'You'd been stubborn and foolish. I had no qualms at exploiting the situation – for my need, Joanne, is greater than yours.'

Bewilderedly she spread her hands, but made no further request for information. It was futile. If he ever thought better of it he would enlighten her, but that would be in his own good time, and for the present Joanne accepted the situation as it was.

'You asked me to stay until Leonor and Filipa go back to their mother. Shall I still be remaining for just that period?'

'By the time my sister is ready to take her children my hopes will have materialized,' he replied enigmatically.

'The position's going to be difficult,' she warned, 'when I'm so completely in the dark.'

'Difficulty will only occur if you create it,' he returned

without much interest. 'No one is going to question the validity of our engagement, and all that's necessary is, as I've said, that you show me a little affection whenever we are in the company of others.' His dark eyes encountered hers and he smiled. 'I too shall behave as if I . . . love you.'

Her blush deepened, and a nervousness assailed her. Unconsciously she twisted her hands in her lap, recalling how Dom Manoel's touch had so disturbed her when they had danced together at Leonor's party. To act as if she cared . . . ? And to have him do the same. Her nervousness increased to real fear, for no matter what Dom Manoel said, she knew her role would prove far more difficult than he believed.

He announced the engagement at dinner the following Sunday. His mother and stepfather were present, and a stunned silence followed when, on taking Joanne's hand, he had given the news in his customary firm clear accents.

'You're – you're going to marry a *widow*!' exclaimed his mother without any effort at tact, and she added incredulously, 'But you hardly know Mrs. Barrie!'

Flushing hotly, Joanne lowered her head, but not before she had seen the dangerous glint that had entered the eyes of her fiancé.

'Joanne and I have known each other for several months – quite long enough to fall in love,' he said abruptly.

Rosa, visibly shaken by his announcement, collected herself together with surprising rapidity. She even managed a smile as she offered her congratulations. Joanne was forced to glance up; Rosa's smile was superficial . . . the hatred in her eyes went very deep. As on one or two previous occasions her attention seemed to be concentrated on the wedding ring Joanne wore, and again Joanne wondered what she was thinking. Could it be that Rosa suspected she was not married? If this were the case Rosa was naturally wondering how Joanne would explain when the time came for her marriage to Dom Manoel to take place. Impatiently Joanne shrugged off her musings. She had no proof that Rosa's thoughts were running on those lines; and in any case, as there would be no marriage, Joanne had nothing to fear. Nevertheless, she bitterly regretted her deception, though precisely for what reason she could not have said.

Manoel and his stepfather were looking at one another, and there was a most odd expression on the older man's face.

'I hope you'll both be very happy,' he murmured on a distinctly satirical note. 'Er – when is the wedding to be?'

His wife glared at him before casting an almost baleful glance in Joanne's direction.

'There's no hurry, Pedro. No matter what Manoel says, they scarcely know one another.'

'But if they're in love,' he mildly returned, his eyes still fixing those of his stepson, 'then what is there to wait for?'

What would they all say, wondered Joanne, when it was known that the wedding would not take place? And how was Manoel to explain? She would have thought a broken engagement would be most abhorrent to him, but there obviously must be one.

'It's early yet to fix the date,' Manoel replied calmly. 'It will be announced in due course.'

Senhor Pedro gave him an expressive glance, but pursued the matter no further. His wife, however, said again there was no need for haste, and a faint smile touched Joanne's lips. So disappointed, Dona Clementina, and so anxious for a delay so that her son might have time to reconsider his decision to marry a widow, and a commoner. Little did she know just how necessary her fears were!

During the meal, which to Joanne was far from pleasant, she several times encountered a vindictive gleam in Rosa's eyes, but there was something else there, something that threatened. Rosa had hoped to marry her cousin, and although she still preserved that air of resignation which had followed her remarkable recovery after Manoel's announcement, her mind seemed to be working furiously and Joanne gained the impression that she wasn't resigned at all. She might be devising some form of villainy, the way she looked, thought Joanne, and then gave herself a mental shake. She seemed always to be imagining things where Rosa was concerned.

The news of the engagement spread quickly and immediately on hearing of it Ricardo rang Joanne up. Manoel answered the phone, and regarded Joanne with a rather odd expression as he said,

'For you – someone by the name of Ricardo.' His voice was crisp and cold, she thought, and wondered if he considered she were taking a liberty by having a friend ring her up at his house.

Ricardo sounded as if he couldn't believe his ears when Joanne said, in answer to his incredulous inquiry,

'Yes, Ricardo, I'm engaged to Dom Manoel.' She had not stopped to think, when she agreed to Manoel's proposal, what effect her engagement would have on Ricardo. And now she felt miserable because she knew he was hurt. Should she tell him the truth? Her first impulse was to do so, but after a little consideration she decided against it. She could not be sure Ricardo would keep it to himself; he was very close to his mother and Joanne suspected he told her everything. No, to enlighten Ricardo would be taking a risk, and Joanne felt a tingle of apprehension at the idea of Manoel's anger if this obscure plan of his were to fail through any fault of hers.

'There's something I don't understand,' exclaimed Ricardo angrily. 'You can't possibly be in love with him!' Joanne made no comment and Ricardo went on, 'I saw you less than a week ago and you didn't say anything about it then!'

She had met him after putting Glee to bed, and he had taken her to his home. Only a few days previously she and Glee had a meal with Ricardo and his mother. On neither occasion had she even mentioned Dom Manoel, so she could understand how odd it must seem to Ricardo that their engagement had now been announced.

'It must seem strange,' she admitted, realizing, to her astonishment, that Manoel was still in the room.

'Strange? It's just not feasible!'

87

'It's – it's quite true,' she reaffirmed, her colour rising now as Manoel glanced up from the book he was supposedly scanning.

'Look here, Joanne, when can I see you?' Ricardo's voice was raised and Joanne looked rather fearfully at Manoel, sure that he was catching every word.

'I can't say – that is—'

'We've been good friends,' he cut in sharply, 'and I want some sort of an explanation, for I'm positive there is an explanation!'

'Perhaps next week some time,' she began, when Ricardo interrupted her.

'What about tonight?'

'No, not tonight; you see, Glee—'

'Glee's taken care of, you've said so yourself.' And, in a softer, persuasive tone, 'Tonight, Joanne, please.'

She bit her lip, wondering what she would say to him. But there would have to be a meeting, for as he had said, they had been good friends. Might as well make it this evening, she decided, and told him she would be at the gate at eight o'clock.

'The gate there – at Dom Manoel's house?'

'Yes – at eight.' Ricardo agreed and thankfully Joanne replaced the receiver. Manoel was standing by the window, the book in his hand. Turning, he let his eyes wander slowly over her, while his brow creased in a frown.

'You've made a man friend since coming here?' he asked shortly.

'Yes, Ricardo Lopes. He lives just along the road from the village.' Why this awkwardness, this tinge of apprehension at the way Manoel was regarding her?

'You're meeting him this evening?'

'That's right.'

'Outside my house?'

Joanne frowned, her temper rising. She resented these questions.

'It doesn't really matter where we meet,' she returned, a hint of tartness in her voice.

'It matters a great deal. I prefer you not to be seen out with this young man at all during the period of our engagement.'

'Are you giving me an order?' she inquired, with a slight toss of her head.

'I'm requesting you to consider my feelings.'

Joanne blinked at him.

'How can my friendship for Ricardo affect your feelings?' she asked, puzzled.

'Use your common sense,' he snapped. 'You're supposed to be in love with *me*! The whole idea of our becoming engaged is to give the impression that we're in love.'

'To give the impression to whom?' Joanne eyed him expectantly, but all she received was a curt reminder that it was none of her business. And she retaliated by the pronouncement that she was definitely going out with Ricardo.

'I think not,' he said with dangerous quiet. 'I won't be made the object of ridicule. Were you to keep company with this Ricardo gossip would naturally result.'

She hadn't thought of that, but now it was pointed out to her she admitted that, in fairness to Manoel, she must practise discretion, and although she still resented his arbitrary tones and manner she agreed to ring Ricardo and make other arrangements.

'Where can I see him?' She looked to Manoel for some suggestion – and saw his mouth tighten as if for a moment he contemplated forbidding her to see Ricardo at all. A militant sparkle entered her eyes as she waited challengingly for him to speak. His own eyes kindled on noting her expression and despite the alteration in her opinion of him Joanne knew that basically he had not changed. The softness and compassion she had discovered merely formed another side to his nature; the arrogance and superiority remained and would come into evidence just whenever he considered they were suited to the occasion. However, to Joanne's surprise his expression relaxed and he said she could ask Ricardo to the house.

'He can come here?' She gazed at him blankly, unable to believe her ears.

'It will be more circumspect for you to meet him here,' he said, but added, 'Tomorrow evening, though.'

'Not tonight?'

'Not tonight.'

Baffled, Joanne asked him why Ricardo could not come this evening.

'Because I say so.'

Her chin came up, but before she had time to make the protesting retort that rose to her lips the door opened and the three children burst into the room.

'Uncle Manoel, will you make an argument for us?' asked Leonor.

'*Settle* an argument,' corrected Glee, laughing.

'Yes – will you, Uncle Manoel?'

'If I can – although you deserve a scolding. Do you usually enter a room in this hooligan fashion?' Leonor shook her head, murmuring an apology. 'What is this argument I'm called upon to settle?'

'It's the bridesmaids,' Filipa put in. 'Leonor says she should be the chief bridesmaid because she's the eldest, and Glee says it should be her because it's her mummy who's getting married.'

A little silence followed these words. Manoel's glance flickered to Joanne; she flushed and lowered her head.

'It isn't important at present,' Manoel said calmly. 'We can talk about it some other time.'

'Oh, but we want to know.' Glee looked at him with that coaxing air and when he ignored her she moved closer and took his hand. 'It should be me, shouldn't it, Uncle Manoel?'

Joanne gave a little gasp and said hastily,

'Dom Manoel, if you please, Glee.'

'But he's my uncle now,' declared Glee, looking to him for support.

'Not yet, Glee,' he smiled. 'But you may call me Uncle if it pleases you.' She treated him to a dazzling smile and his

90

lips twitched in amusement. Watching him, Joanne experienced that odd disturbance again, but before she had time to dwell on it, or to analyse it, Glee was speaking, insisting on an answer to her question.

'I've said, Glee, that it isn't important just now.' Disengaging his hand, he waved it towards the door. 'Off you go, all of you – and close the door *quietly* behind you!'

'Their English has improved enormously,' he said when they had gone, and Joanne flushed at the praise.

'They could speak it quite well before,' she submitted modestly.

'Still of the opinion that you're not earning your money, eh?'

'Let's not pretend, Manoel,' she returned, a laugh in her voice.

'Nevertheless, I still maintain you've done some good work with Filipa and Leonor.'

He was in a most approachable mood and Joanne said daringly,

'Will you buy my farm – some time?'

His eyes travelled to the window, and to the clutter of ugly buildings spoiling his view.

'I'll buy your farm, Joanne. Have no fear, you've not lost all your money.'

Joanne examined his profile, noting the firm and finely-chiselled lines of the aristocrat, the aquiline nose and thrusting jaw. The thick black hair, waving slightly from his dark forehead, had a sprinkling of grey at the temples, giving him an even more distinguished appearance. Truly he was very different from any man she had ever known. He turned his head and as she became aware of his amused stare she coloured, put out as much by his attention as by the sudden fluttering of her pulse.

'It's ... very good of you,' she murmured gratefully, hoping her confusion was not so apparent that he would perceive it.

'Not at all,' he objected. 'I've always wanted the land, as you already know.' He spoke quietly, and with an honesty that strengthened the accessibility of his mood. 'I must confess, Joanne, I was very angry when you wouldn't sell, but as it's turned out, it was all for the best.'

'The best?'

'Had you sold me the farm, either when I saw you in England or later, when I made you the offer, you wouldn't be here now, assisting me with my problem.'

'You blackmailed me,' she accused, at the same time wondering at this problem and wishing he would confide in her.

'It was the only way,' he said, offering no apology. 'I wanted you to come here, for it was my intention that we should become engaged.'

'Even at the time of Glee's accident?'

He frowned and said a trifle shortly,

'Glee's accident helped my plan, but I don't want you to misunderstand, or to misjudge me. Glee's welfare, and your peace of mind, were of the first importance. The only sensible course was to have you both here, where Glee could have expert care, and where you would be relieved of the work and worry of the farm.'

'It was good of you,' she said again, and his frown deepened.

'It was my duty. I did mention that we're related.'

She shook her head.

'You'd have helped me had we not been related.'

'Perhaps, but we'll let that pass.' The humorous gleam entered his eyes again as he added, 'Don't give me too much credit, Joanne. I did want something in return, remember.'

He baffled her, for hadn't he just said his first concern had been for the welfare of both Glee and herself?

'I hope that what I'm doing will amply repay you.' There was a persuasive element in her tone, inviting confidence. Noting it, Manoel said, rather gently,

'Naturally you're puzzled, Joanne, but I can't confide in you. Just accept the position without question – consider your engagement to me as a task, a task which you are performing to help me, and to please me.' He paused, raising a questioning eyebrow as the colour began to fluctuate in Joanne's cheeks and her hands twitched nervously in her lap. What was not so evident was the sudden quickening of her heartbeats, and that strangely disturbing sensation which was becoming both familiar and uncomfortable. 'When the engagement has served its purpose you'll be free to return to England – having been paid for your farm, of course.'

She thought about his saying that the materialization of his hopes should coincide with the return of Filipa and Leonor to their mother. Everyone would be gone from the Solar de Alvares except Manoel and his cousin. The idea brought Joanne a feeling of dejection and she frowned in thought as she endeavoured to account for it. But no explanation presented itself and Joanne decided she was miserable simply because she would miss the two children. Glee, too, would miss them, for the three had become great friends. At home, Glee had naturally had her little companions, but here Leonor and Filipa were more like her sisters. Glee was going to experience a painful wrench on being parted from them. A deep sigh rose to Joanne's lips and Manoel eyed her quizzically.

'What was that for?' he demanded. 'Is it that you can't curb your curiosity?'

'Of course not. I'm quite resigned to being kept in the dark.'

'But you don't like it?' He actually laughed then. 'How typically feminine you are!' Recovering from her dejection, Joanne searched for some suitable retort, but before she could find one Manoel spoke again, changing the subject. 'I don't know how deep your friendship for this young man is, Joanne, but I take it you're not in love with him?'

Joanne flushed and shook her head.

'No . . . I don't think so.'

He frowned. 'You're not sure?'

'I am sure,' she said after a small hesitation. 'I'm not in love with Ricardo.'

'Good, then it won't be difficult to convince him that

you're in love with me.'

'Oh, but—' She had been racking her brains to think of some explanation to give Ricardo, and finally decided there was only one course open to her – to tell him the truth, but only after extracting a promise of secrecy from him.

'But what, Joanne?' His voice was crisp, inflexible. She knew Manoel would not countenance her confiding in Ricardo.

'What can I say to him? You see, we're very good friends, and – and he knows I'm not in love with you.'

'How can he know that?'

Joanne spread her hands helplessly. 'I haven't ever said anything about – about liking you.'

'Perhaps you've said something about disliking me,' he challenged, sending her into renewed confusion. His eyes flickered perceptively and he went on to say she would simply have to disillusion Ricardo, and own to having fallen in love with Manoel himself.

'It'll be quite impossible.'

'Nonsense! You've fallen in love with me suddenly. It often happens.'

'No, I can't—'

'You will, Joanne,' he said, very softly. 'As I've said, I'll not be the object of ridicule. You'll oblige me by convincing this friend of yours that our engagement is genuine.' And without giving her time for further protest he glanced at the clock and rose from his chair, saying he had work to do. The next moment Joanne was alone, her mind in a turmoil as once again she tried to think what she would say to Ricardo.

A few minutes before Ricardo was due to arrive Manoel came up to Joanne in her sitting-room. She had just put Glee to bed and was setting out some refreshments on the table.

'One thing I forgot to mention,' he said coolly. 'I don't want Rosa to know this friend of yours has been here this evening. Please see that you don't mention it to her.'

'Rosa? But I don't understand?' Rosa was out, visiting a friend, and Joanne now saw why it was that Manoel had made her change the date of Ricardo's visit. Last evening Rosa was at home.

'Once again I'm unable to give you a reason. Have I your word?'

'I won't mention it to Rosa, no, not if you say I mustn't. But—'

'Thank you, Joanne.' He turned at the door, his glance straying to the table. 'Have a pleasant evening.'

She smiled swiftly in response, having, as on a previous occasion, a rather urgent desire to keep him with her.

'If you're not doing anything – later – perhaps you'd join us?'

But he shook his head.

'I've some work to do; it'll take me the whole evening.'

'Oh. . . .' Still the desire remained and she went on to ask if he were starting his work immediately.

'Immediately,' he replied, watching her with amused curiosity. Could he possibly know she was trying to keep him? wondered Joanne with some dismay. If he did, he had no intention of obliging, for after another glance at the table he turned and left the room.

Joanne stared at the closed door, her mind in a turmoil. Why had she wanted him to stay? – and why this strange emptiness now he had gone?

Ricardo came a few moments later and for a tensed second or two they stared at one another.

'Sit d-down, Ricardo,' she invited, her voice not quite steady. 'Will you have a drink?'

'Joanne—' He strode across the room and took her by the shoulders. 'What the dickens is going on? This engagement – there's something fishy about it, because you're not in love with Dom Manoel.'

Joanne gave him a rather dazed look, and even as she realized his intention, and made to break away from his hold, Ricardo had kissed her hard on the mouth.

'Ricardo!' she gasped, twisting out of his arms. 'You

shouldn't have done that!'

'Why not?' he demanded angrily. 'Tell me about this phoney engagement. What's the reason for it?'

Joanne turned from him, her whole body quivering.

'There's usually only one reason for an engagement,' she whispered in trembling tones.

'When people get engaged they're usually in love!' was Ricardo's grim response. 'But nothing you can say will convince me you're in love with Dom Manoel!'

Slowly she came round to face him, and he saw that the colour had left her cheeks.

'I'm afraid you'll have to be convinced, Ricardo,' she said gently. 'For it's true – I do love Dom Manoel.'

CHAPTER SIX

IT had been so easy, at the time, for Joanne to promise to remain at the Solar de Alvares until she was no longer needed, but as the days went by she began to wonder if the time would come when she would find it impossible to keep that promise. It was not just that she was thrown more and more into Manoel's company, owing to their engagement, but his manner towards her held all the tender affection of the lover. Not that he was over-demonstrative — Joanne felt he would never be that, even with the woman he would eventually marry — but he was gentle with her and anxious about her welfare. Sometimes his mother and stepfather were there, but for the most part Rosa was the only witness, and it was soon impressed into Joanne that his attentiveness was for her benefit only. What did it all mean? Was it revenge for something Rosa had done? Was his object to make her jealous? No explanation that Joanne could think up satisfied her and she eventually abandoned the effort of trying to unravel the mystery. But Manoel's assumed tenderness disturbed her profoundly; if only he could mean it. . . . But that would never be, and she hastily dismissed the thought.

Every week Manoel went to see his sister in the hospital at Lisbon, and one day when he was out Rosa came up to the sitting-room which Joanne still retained. Her eyes were dark with jealousy and hate, yet there was a certain air of triumph about her that had the effect of setting Joanne's nerves on edge. Several times during the last couple of days Joanne had caught Rosa glancing oddly at her, and now Rosa came straight to the point, inquiring curtly when the wedding was to be.

Joanne shrugged carelessly, but her flesh tingled. She felt she would never have the courage to face Manoel, should she make a slip.

'We haven't yet fixed the date.'

An ugly twist totally transformed Rosa's face; she looked actually wicked, thought Joanne.

'Is there to be a wedding?' inquired Rosa in soft and purring tones.

'What a thing to ask!'

Rosa threw her a flickering glance from under her lashes.

'Are you contemplating bigamy, by any chance?' Lazily she took possession of a chair and leant back comfortably in it.

'Bigamy?' Joanne gaped at her. 'Did you say bigamy?'

'How well you do it,' sneered the Portuguese girl triumphantly. 'You're not a widow, are you, Joanne?'

Joanne went taut. How did Rosa know that?

'You're not being very explicit, Rosa.'

'I've been speaking to your daughter,' admitted Rosa without the least sign of shame. 'Her daddy isn't dead.' Joanne's eyes flickered contemptuously over her, but her mind worked furiously. There must be a way out of this, she thought, realizing that Rosa had deliberately waited until Manoel was absent from the house, so that there would be no risk of his walking in on them unexpectedly.

'You're despicable!' Joanne still searched frantically for some means of escape. The other girl subjected her to a mildly indifferent stare as she said,

'My action's not nearly so despicable as yours in deceiving Manoel like this. Would you really go to the lengths of marrying him?'

'I'm not willing to discuss our marriage with you,' responded Joanne stiffly.

'I'll bet you're not!' Rosa stood up, and walked languidly to the door, for Joanne was standing, in an attitude of impatience. 'Naturally I shall pass on my knowledge to Manoel, for I can't sit back and see him made to appear such an utter fool.'

Joanne bit her lip, cursing herself for the stubbornness that had prevented her from putting Manoel in possession of the facts. Truly this was a 'web of lies' in which by her obstinacy she had become enmeshed. If Rosa were to carry out her threat then Manoel would have no alternative but to call the engagement off and whatever plan he had in mind must fail. That Rosa would carry out her threat there was nothing so sure ... unless Joanne could devise some means of preventing her.

'Be careful you yourself aren't made to appear a fool,' she warned, taking the only way that might prove fruitful. 'One must be very sure of one's facts before making accusations that might not be true.' Something in her tone brought Rosa round with a jerk, her face paling slightly.

'How can I appear a fool?'

'As I've just said – by repeating what might not be true.'

'You mean – you are a widow?'

'So you're beginning to doubt the dependability of what you've heard from so young a child as Glee?'

A sneer curved Rosa's mouth.

'Do you think I'd fall for your bluff?' she asked with a hint of contempt. 'I'm not quite such a fool as that.'

Joanne's hand fluttered in a little careless gesture. But it was a matter of wonderment to her that she could speak in so steady a voice.

'Go ahead then, and give your information to Manoel.'

A frown crossed Rosa's brow; she scrutinized Joanne intently.

'Glee mentioned her father—' Rosa shook her head. 'I know you're not a widow!'

'Really,' said Joanne with some impatience, 'would any woman in her right mind contemplate marriage if she were not free to marry?'

'You're telling me you are in fact a widow?'

'I don't make a practice of discussing my private life,' replied Joanne in quiet yet decisive tones.

'There's some mystery—' Rosa stopped, her gaze travelling to the lovely ring on Joanne's finger. Naturally she no longer wore her mother's wedding ring, and as she watched Rosa's changing expression Joanne's heartbeats quickened even before the girl spoke, this time in a softly purring voice which in itself was an open threat. 'Perhaps, then, *Mrs.* Barrie, my first suspicion was the correct one. I don't believe you're a widow, and you say yourself you are free to marry, so Glee is . . . is. . . .'

'Yes, Dona Rosa?' prompted Joanne, her lovely eyes kindling dangerously. 'Are you afraid to finish what you were about to say?'

A slight flush tinted Rosa's cheeks, but she remained otherwise unruffled by Joanne's question.

'I don't believe you've ever been married to Glee's father,' she emphatically declared, and Joanne could scarcely contain her laughter. If only she could tell this detestable girl the truth! How very gratifying it would be to witness her humiliating defeat.

'In that case there's no barrier to my marriage to Manoel,' was all she said, and once again she had difficulty in suppressing her amusement, for a look of absolute horror had crossed the other girl's dark face.

'Manoel would never for one moment contemplate marriage to – to a woman who had had a child out of wedlock!' she returned in a shocked yet faintly triumphant tone.

Joanne paused in thought. The situation was serious indeed, but for the moment she was carried away by the more humorous aspect of it and she said carelessly,

'Why not? It happens all the time nowadays. Sensible people accept such things. I can't see that Manoel will trouble himself overmuch about my past.' And she added, allowing her glance to flicker over Rosa's slim figure in a deliberately significant sort of way, 'I daresay Manoel's had his amours, but—' she shrugged indifferently – 'his past is no concern of mine. I'd never be so presumptuous as to question him about it.' If Manoel could hear all this! In spite of her amusement Joanne gave an involuntary shudder. She had never witnessed his anger, and she hoped she never would – for his impatience was quite disconcerting enough.

Rosa's heightened colour gave evidence of her fury.

'You're insolent! How dare you insinuate—? Oh, wait until I tell Manoel about this – and I shall tell him, for I'm quite sure he doesn't know what he's doing in contemplating marriage to a shameless woman like you!'

Her words brought Joanne back with a jerk to the seriousness of the situation and she dropped her bantering manner.

'What are you going to say to Manoel?' she inquired curiously.

'I'm going to repeat what you've just admitted.'

'And what have I admitted?'

Rosa came back into the room; the two girls stared at one another. Joanne's gaze was unflinching and for one short moment she saw uncertainty in those dark eyes and she seized upon it. 'You've only yourself to blame if I teased you,' she said, adopting a tone of mild apology. 'But if you're honest you'll admit you asked for it.' Would it work? she wondered breathlessly.

'You mean . . . your daughter *is* legitimate?' Rosa lost a little more of her colour – and her confidence.

'Certainly Glee is legitimate!' Thank heaven for the chance to speak without dissembling for once, thought Joanne with heartfelt relief. 'Be very careful you don't slander me, Rosa.'

'Slander—?' A long pause, and then Rosa's lips snapped together. 'You're not a widow! Glee saw her father, recently.'

Joanne's heartbeats quickened. How could she stop this girl from passing on her suspicions to Manoel? That the girl was muddled was evident, but whatever she chose to say to Manoel would result in his demanding an explanation. On the one hand, it would be an overwhelming relief to unburden herself of this weight of guilt – but on the other hand Joanne had an equally overwhelming aversion to finding herself the victim of her fiancé's wrath. And that he would be furious she had not the slightest doubt, for her revelation would make him appear a complete fool before his mother and stepfather who would be sure to look askance at such a stupid and unnecessary deception. That stubborn streak in her nature would get her into trouble one day, her mother had repeatedly said ... and how right she had proved to be!

'Did you put the words into Glee's mouth in the same way as when you were talking about the accident?' inquired Joanne, outwardly calm, but speaking in desperation for all that. 'On that particular occasion you managed to get her to say what you wanted, so you've probably done the same again.' She paused, then added deliberately, 'If I were you, Rosa, I'd keep quiet, for Manoel might take it into his head to question Glee ... and other things could just come to light.' It was a desperate move, and in normal circumstances it would have been an unfair one. But with an adversary like Rosa the most effective weapon had to be used. Rosa was staring at her, now plainly off balance, and Joanne added for good measure, 'I'm really surprised at a woman of your intelligence taking a child so young as Glee seriously. If you had the least understanding of children you'd know that at her particular age they indulge in much fantasy. It's part of their normal development and quite often they invent relations. Glee used to invent sisters – and actually talked to them and played with them – until we came here and she found companions in Filipa and Leonor.' This last was perfectly true, and the sincerity with which Joanne was able to speak strengthened her argument. Rosa's face turned a sickly yellow and Joanne felt a surge of relief sweep over her at the knowledge that she had defeated the Portuguese girl. Rosa would now think twice before running to Manoel with suspicions which she would have to admit were based entirely upon what Glee had told her.

But Joanne's peace of mind was to be short-lived, for less than a week later, while they were all having dinner together, Rosa declared her intention of taking a holiday in England. Her gaze was fixed darkly on Joanne as she spoke.

'Why England?' The question was out before Joanne had time to think, for Rosa's information had shaken her.

'I met an English family while on holiday last year, and they invited me to visit them.' Rosa turned to her cousin, who was sitting next to her at the table. 'Do you remember my mentioning them, Manoel?'

He nodded.

'I do recall your telling me about them, yes.' He paused in thought. 'They live somewhere in the Midlands, I think you said?'

'Not far from Birmingham.' She smiled at Joanne and purred, 'How far is that from your home, Joanne?'

A tingling sensation took possession of Joanne's whole body.

'I lived near Northampton,' she supplied, picking up a roll and breaking it with hands that were shaking slightly.

'Not too far from where I'll be staying. I must do some travelling around. I expect my friends will take me about in their car.'

'When are you thinking of going, Rosa?' asked Manoel, and Joanne looked quickly at him. Was it imagination, or was there a hint of satisfaction in his voice?

'Immediately after Christmas.' She glanced at Joanne. 'Not the best time to visit your country, I'm told?'

'Just about the worst.' Joanne leant back in her chair as Mafalda smilingly took her empty plate. 'It can be very cold in England at that time of the year.'

'Never mind. It isn't as if I'm going for a normal holiday. It's more to see these friends than anything else.' She spoke lightly, but Joanne read a deeper meaning into her words. An uneasiness enveloped her and she found her appetite had gone.

'How long will you be away?' Manoel looked at Rosa inquiringly and her lips suddenly tightened.

'Not long. A week, perhaps.'

'Only a week?' His brows lifted. 'Hardly worth going for.'

Joanne gave a little inaudible gasp. Where was Manoel's customary suave tact? His words and manner gave the impression that he actually desired Rosa to be away for a longer period. Rosa gained the same impression, for a hint of angry colour fused her cheeks.

'A week will be quite long enough for what I want to do,' she said between her teeth.

Manoel frowned and looked up. Rosa's eyes were on Joanne, and Manoel also turned his attention to her. She lowered her head, for she knew there was an expression of fear in her eyes. What did Rosa mean? She was going to England to see her friends, she said, but Joanne now felt convinced there was some other motive for her visit. . . .

A little later, frowning at the small portion of meat on her plate, Manoel said anxiously,

'What's wrong, Joanne? Aren't you hungry?'

She shook her head, avoiding Rosa's gaze – and the smirk of satisfaction that she instinctively knew had come to her lips.

'Not very, Manoel.'

'You're quite well, dear?'

She smiled then, and nodded.

'It's just that I'm not hungry. There's nothing else the matter with me.'

After dinner Rosa went to her room, and later went out, saying she was visiting a friend who lived further down the valley. Her car crunched along the drive as Manoel and Joanne were sitting in the salon, listening to the soft music coming from the record player. Manoel's ears seemed to be strained to hear the last purr of the engine. His eyes were hard and his jaw set. What was this mystery? Joanne mused with swift impatience. Why couldn't he be more informative—? She pulled herself up with a jerk, reflecting with a shock that she was not his fiancée and, therefore, his actions were no business of hers. Not his fiancée. . . . So odd, but with every passing day she became more and more used to the idea of being engaged in the real sense of the word, and she could not visualize the time when she would no longer be the object of his gentleness and affection. Assumed, these were, of course, and should have meant nothing at all to her – just as the attentions he received from her meant nothing to him – but every little look and word, every smile of apparent tenderness, these meant everything to Joanne; memories to be carefully stored and treasured. He would never know, she thought, and a wistfulness entered her eyes that brought a sudden frown to Manoel's brow.

'Joanne dear, you're not well, I can see it.'

Dear. . . . Why did he torture her? There was no one here to deceive.

'I'm quite well,' she insisted, managing a smile. 'Don't worry about me, Manoel.'

'But I must worry about you.' He smiled, and the torture increased. Why that particular smile? – the smile that had so attracted her, and given her the first faint inkling that her heart was no longer her own. 'There's no one else to worry about you – at least, not here in Portugal.'

His concern was natural, she supposed, for in a way he had taken both Glee and herself under his protection for the duration of their stay in his house.

'You're kind, Manoel,' she said faintly, embarrassment sweeping over her. 'I'm just a little tired, perhaps.'

'Have the children been trying?'

'Not at all. They're wonderful pupils.'

'How does that rascal of yours go on at the school here?'

Joanne laughed.

'Nothing worries Glee. She's most adaptable.'

'So I've noticed,' he responded ruefully. 'She's fitted in here as if she's one of the family. I've heard you once or twice telling her not to call me Uncle, but I wouldn't bother if I were you, Joanne, for she's quite determined to adopt me as her uncle.'

Yes, thought Joanne, her mind going back to those times when her mother had made a persistent effort to force Glee to refer to Joanne as her aunt. But Glee had made up her mind – and when Glee made up her mind no amount of persuasion could change it.

'She's going to miss it all when we leave,' murmured Joanne wistfully, thinking also of herself. 'Glee's never had companions like Filipa and Leonor.'

'She's been lonely, you mean?'

'Not that exactly. But an only child misses such a lot – the company of other children in the home, mainly.'

The music stopped and Manoel rose, going over to the record player with the intention of putting on another record. There was something strange in his manner and Joanne felt he had been affected by the conversation. He had grown extraordinarily fond of Glee, as she had of him. Could it be, then, that he too would experience a sense of loss on their departure?

He hesitated, as if undecided whether or not to play the record; Joanne watched him in profile, noting the clear-cut lines and the noble thrust of his chin. Magnificent seemed the only fitting description and with a little self-deprecating sigh Joanne wondered at her foolishness in falling in love with such a man. He turned, the record still in his hand, and surprised a look of wistfulness in her eyes. Replacing the record in the rack, he came back across the room and stood there, looking down at her for a moment.

'What is it, Joanne?' he inquired gently. 'You've not been yourself for the past hour or so.'

She glanced up, forcing a smile. It would be difficult to keep anything from him, she thought, again asserting there was nothing wrong with her.

'You're quiet . . . and so pale. Perhaps a little fresh air is what you need. Go and fetch your coat and we'll take a walk.'

Stunned by his words, Joanne just sat there staring incredulously at him. Even had Rosa been present there was no need to carry his concern to these lengths.

'Do you really want to go for a walk?' she queried doubtfully.

'It's a lovely evening. You're not too tired?' And when she shook her head, 'Then fetch your coat,' he repeated, and she hurried away, her mind in a turmoil.

Could this be acting? His concern for her seemed very real. . . .

They strolled through the grounds, with the air around them moving gently, pine-scented and soft as thistledown. High above, tiny pools of silver glistened from a dome of purple velvet. As they walked the moon came up, then a film of ivory cloud appeared, gliding and swaying so that it seemed as if the moon were drowsily sailing across the sky, unfolding its light as it went and shedding a pearl-like splendour over the entire landscape. No sound intruded into the vast stillness and Joanne was impressed with a profound sense of unreality. To be strolling like this with the man she had so intensely disliked, the man whose pompous mien and haughty mode of address had so irritated her that she had stubbornly refused to rectify his mistake – the mistake which at present was causing her such trouble and anxiety. And now she knew only pleasure at his voice, experienced a sort of exquisite pain when in his presence.

She uttered a deep, appreciative sigh, determined to cast off these depressing musings and take advantage of what was offered.

'You were right, Manoel; it's a lovely evening.'

'You have it cooler than this in England at this time of the year.' It was a statement and she asked if he had been to England during the winter, realizing just how little she knew about him. But then these were the first moments of real intimacy they had shared. 'Yes, I've been at this time of the year.'

'And stayed in London, of course,' she said with a laugh.

'What makes you so sure of that?'

'All foreigners who go to England stay in London.'

'It's a wonderful city,' he returned reflectively. 'There isn't anywhere in the world quite like it.'

She slackened her pace, and half turned towards him.

'What is the particular attraction?' she wanted to know, eyeing him curiously.

The question gave him cause for thought.

'The atmosphere, mainly. But you have the buildings, and the river – there's always something different about a town situated on a river,' he added, still in a mood of reflection. 'And, I think, its past. In London you have with you always the sense of history.' They had reached the lake and Manoel took Joanne's hand and led her to the seat under a tree by the shore. The lake was large, and waves lapped gently at their feet.

It was some seconds before Joanne realized her hand was still in his and, with a hasty, awkward movement she withdrew it. He smiled faintly at her action, but made no comment. He appeared completely at his ease, leaning back on the seat and staring absently into the gleaming waters of the lake. In contrast, Joanne felt tensed and uncomfortable, sitting upright on the edge of the seat and twisting her hands convulsively in her lap.

Becoming aware of this uneasiness, Manoel looked curiously at her hands for a while, then said, in that quiet attractive voice of his,

'Sit back, Joanne, and relax. What is the matter with you this evening?'

Obediently she leant back against the support and after a little while Manoel began asking about her people in England.

'You have a brother, I know, but have you any other relatives?'

'A sister, Chris. She's married, but has no children yet.'

'Ah, yes; I heard you mention her, but I didn't meet her.'

'I suppose I should have introduced you to her,' she owned, biting her lip. 'I'm afraid,' she added regretfully, 'that my manners were far from perfect on the occasion of your visit to me in England.'

'I suppose my manners will be lacking if I agree with you,' he responded with some amusement, and she had to laugh.

'Nevertheless, you do agree with me?'

He nodded, and turned towards her, a faint smile on his lips.

'Honestly should always rank above diplomacy.'

'In that case I must be honest too?'

'Most certainly,' he encouraged, and she responded, although with slight hesitancy,

'It was your attitude.'

'My attitude?' he frowned. 'You took exception to it?'

Joanne paused, then said in a voice edged with mirth,

'Perhaps I'll settle for diplomacy after all.'

His eyes were searching.

'I'll have honesty, if you please.' A sudden order, that, and Joanne ruefully wished she had never introduced the subject.

'I – I found you a little – unfriendly.' That was certainly putting it mildly, and in spite of herself an involuntary gleam of amusement entered her eyes.

Manoel looked perceptively at her and demanded a fuller explanation.

'This is the first time anyone has ever accused me of discourtesy,' he added in crisp and acid tones.

'Oh, you weren't discourteous,' she hastily denied. 'It was just that – that—' She broke off, shaking her head. 'I can't explain, Manoel, so please let the matter drop.'

But he meant to have the explanation and Joanne had no alternative but to enlighten him as to the sort of impression he had made upon her at their first meeting. She spoke with care and tact, but his dark eyes were kindling dangerously when at last she fell silent.

'So you regarded me as an arrogant snob, full of my own importance—!'

'No – oh, no! I never said *that*!'

'But you implied it!'

Joanne turned unhappily, her eyes clouding.

'I'm sorry. I do realize now that I was mistaken – what I mean is, I gained a totally wrong impression of you.' She shook her head, thoughtful for a moment. 'I can't understand how it happened. Perhaps it was because you were so insistent about the farm.'

'I was certainly keen to buy, but I made you a fair offer. There was no question of my demanding, or taking anything for granted. And if I said you wouldn't be able to make it pay, that was merely good advice, given solely because you appeared so young, and so totally unfitted to take on a place that had been so long neglected.'

'I know that now,' she returned meekly. 'You were right . . . in everything you said.'

Mollified by her admission, Manoel allowed a hint of amusement to enter his voice as he said,

'This impression, then, is to be blamed for your own rather off-hand manner towards me?'

Her lips twitched, for he too was putting it mildly.

'There seems to have been a big misunderstanding all round. We got off to a bad start, though just how I can't remember.'

'It isn't important any more.' He turned from her, contemplating the lake again. It shone like polished silver, for much of the cloud had disappeared and the moon was completely unmasked. 'I suppose we should go in, the breeze appears to be freshening.'

Joanne made no move as she experienced that desire to keep him at her side. What good it would do her she did not know, but every moment was precious, for Manoel had told her yesterday that his sister would be out of hospital for Christmas, and the children would be returning to their own home early in January.

'I'm not cold,' she submitted. 'It's still a beautiful night.'

'I agree it's still a beautiful night; I don't agree that you're not cold. You've just shivered.' He stood up and she had no choice but to do the same. They walked slowly back to the house, through formal gardens and vine-covered arbours, past fountains decorated with blue and yellow *azulejos*, and finally they entered between an avenue of trees whose shadows were darkly thrown across a moonlit lawn.

The house became visible before a backcloth of pines rising in sharp relief against a lustrous sky, its marble façade bathed in an enchanting radiance of cream and pearl. The light was soft, translucent; the disc above shone more brightly as the last remnant of cloud drifted from the sky; with the increase of light magic seemed to be released and Joanne gasped audibly at the beauty around her. Manoel stopped, as if he too appreciated the magic of their surroundings.

'We're so lucky, to be experiencing all this,' Joanne whispered, almost reverently. 'I've never known anything quite like it.' Nor would she ever again, she thought, a little catch of despair rising to mar this, the most unforgettable of the incidents she was so carefully adding to her precious store of memories.

'We are lucky, Joanne,' he agreed and, taking her by the shoulders, he gently turned her round to face him. She looked up, her lips softly parted, her eyes wide and questioning, her heart beating so loudly that she felt sure he must hear it. Manoel stood for a long while, staring down at her, shaking his head now and then as if in amazement at the discovery of things he had not seen before. 'How beautiful you are,' he whispered. 'How perfect in every way.' And with a firm, possessive movement he drew her close, his arms encircling her in a strong yet tender embrace. He bent his dark head and kissed her on the lips. 'Joanne, my dear. . . .' He held her from him, his gaze expectant, as if he wanted to hear her speak. But she was too full, too overcome by sheer happiness. For this wasn't acting; it was no demonstration for Rosa's benefit, but sincere—

'Hello, Rosa, are you out walking too?' Manoel's voice was soft and suave. He released Joanne but retained her hand. 'Like us, you're taking advantage of this wonderful evening.'

She came from behind a clump of bushes, a smile on her lips.

'I got home about ten minutes ago, and felt like a breath of fresh air.'

Joanne had gone rigid, and the colour flooded her face at the memory of the way she had so eagerly responded to her fiancé's kisses, believing them to be sincere. But he had known Rosa was there, strolling along behind the bushes.

'And I should have known there was some reason for his action,' whispered Joanne convulsively. 'How could I be so foolish as to believe he'd fallen in love with me?'

The more she dwelt on it the more she squirmed with shame and humiliation. What must he think? But suddenly a surge of anger swept through her. He had no right to carry his acting that far. She had agreed to pose as his fiancée, it was true, but she had not reckoned on being subjected to Manoel's sham lovemaking. Nor would she endure it; he should be made to see, once and for all, that he must keep his distance.

For the next couple of days she deliberately avoided him as much as possible, using her own sitting-room more than had been her practice of late. And when she did of necessity find herself in his company, as when they all had dinner together in the evening, Joanne saw that her manner was – for Rosa's benefit – friendly, and no more. Hardness in Manoel's eyes she often encountered, but he gave no other visible sign that he noticed any change in her manner towards him. Naturally he would do his utmost to conceal from Rosa any rift that might have developed between Joanne and himself.

On the third morning Joanne received a letter which upset her so much that, after dwelling on its contents for most of the day, she eventually made up her mind to talk to Manoel about it. She sought him out just before dinner; he was in the salon, reading, and glanced up as she entered, his hard eyes sweeping over with indifference, but kindling with faint interest as they finally settled on her face.

'You want something, Joanne?' His voice was cold and crisp. She guessed that he had deliberately spoken first in order to convey his awareness that she would not be approaching him like this unless she did want something. The question was also designed to affect her confidence; it succeeded, and to her annoyance Joanne found herself stammering,

'Manoel, I've had a – a letter from a friend of mine. She's

mother and I — I wondered if you'd mind very ... if I went to her — just for a few days?'

She hadn't been very explicit, and a questioning lift of his brow brought forth some further explanation. Lynn, her friend from their schooldays, had at nineteen given up a promising career in the Civil Service to devote her time to her mother, who had become paralysed. This was seven years ago and now Lynn was left, alone in the great house which her mother had refused to give up. As she had not worked or gone visiting she had no friend to whom she could turn — no friend except Joanne who, before coming to Portugal, had made a practice of visiting Lynn and her mother at least once a week.

'These were the only breaks Lynn ever had,' Joanne went on, watching his expression anxiously. 'She never went out in the evenings, nor even had a holiday. She's feeling terribly lonely and lost, and I must go to her— If you don't mind?' she added on a little pleading note, for it seemed to her that his eyes had taken on a more pronounced hardness even while she spoke.

'She has no other relatives, you say?'

Joanne shook her head.

'Lynn's father died when she was small; she's an only child and hasn't even a distant cousin to whom she could turn.'

A frown crossed Manoel's face; he appeared vaguely troubled, she thought, as he sat there in silence for what seemed an eternity.

'Supposing you did go, for a few days, what could you do for her?'

'Well ... nothing much,' she was bound to admit. 'But Lynn wouldn't feel quite so alone. You see, it's only a week since her mother died, and they were greatly devoted to one another. Lynn must be feeling dreadful.'

A little sigh broke from his lips and again he lapsed into thought.

'If you go to her, and then come away, it will, I'm sure, be worse than not going at all.' His tones were firm, decisive, and Joanne bit her lip. She could insist on g̶o̶ was no reason at all why she should ask Manoel's p̶ mission, but she was after all employed by Manoel and she owed it to him to ask his consent to this absence.

'I'd like to go, Manoel,' she persisted, 'if you don't mind?'

'You'll be coming away about a week before Christmas.'

'Yes. . . .' Joanne hadn't thought of that. 'It's going to be awful for her, having Christmas alone.'

'That's exactly what I've been thinking,' he returned, almost staggering her by the admission. She had told him about Lynn because she was so troubled about her, and because she felt it was her duty to make some effort to go to her; but she had not expected Manoel to bother his head very much about the matter. He looked at her for a thoughtful moment and then said firmly, 'She must come here. Invite her to stay for as long as she likes.'

'She – she can come here?' If she was staggered before Joanne felt completely stunned now. 'But you don't know her!'

'She's your friend, and she happens to be in need, so she must come to you.' A faint smile erased the last hard line from his mouth. 'We're here to help one another, Joanne,' he said quietly, 'and life loses its purpose once we begin to ignore that fact.'

Joanne swallowed a curious little lump that had suddenly lodged in her throat. She forgot how he had used her, causing her shame and humiliation that had naturally brought anger in its wake. For he was a truly wonderful person . . . and yet how deceiving at times when that arrogance was in evidence, and that icy inflection was allowed to creep into his voice.

'It's most kind of you, Manoel,' she quivered, too full to say much. 'I'll let her know right away.'

'Yes, do that. And I've also been thinking . . . she might prefer a little privacy at times, for obviously she won't have got over her sorrow yet. So she can have a bedroom next to your suite, and use your sitting-room. When she doesn't want to be alone she can of course join us down here.'

It was ridiculous to cry, but tears stood on Joanne's lashes, and her voice was husky with emotion as she thanked him again.

'If she just stays over Christmas,' she began, when he interrupted her.

'She must stay as long as she likes,' he repeated firmly.

'You mean – she can stay until Glee and I go back to England? We could then leave together—'

'We'll talk about your going home another time,' he cut in sharply, and Joanne looked at him in surprise – not only because of the marked change in his voice, but also because his manner conveyed the impression that even the mention of their leaving here angered him.

'You said the children would be returning to their own home early in January,' she reminded him breathlessly.

'Well?' Slight arrogance in the lift of his brow and the hardness had returned to his eyes.

'I expected to be leaving. ... My services won't be necessary.'

'You and I happen to be engaged – or have you forgotten?'

Was he making a subtle reference to her avoidance of him? she wondered, blinking at him, her mind confused.

'You said our engagement would last only until the children left here.'

'I believe I did.' He stifled a yawn and glanced down to where he had placed his book on the couch beside him. 'I should communicate with your friend immediately, Joanne. She's sure to be anxiously awaiting your reply to her letter.' Picking up his book, Manoel began to read. Joanne stared at him for a moment, her mind more confused than ever by his deliberate dropping of the subject.

'I'll tell her to come, then. Will someone bring her from the airport?'

He glanced up.

'Certainly; I'll send the car.'

'Thank you, Manoel,' she said, and quietly left the room.

CHAPTER SEVEN

HELENA and Joanne were strangely attracted to one another right from the start, and when on bringing his sister home a week before Christmas Manoel had introduced Joanne as his fiancée, Helena greeted her with undisguised enthusiasm.

'I couldn't wait to see you,' she smiled, her big brown eyes wandering over Joanne's slim figure and then coming to rest admiringly on her face. 'Manoel always did have excellent taste!'

Naturally Joanne blushed. Rosa was present and her eyes darkened with suppressed fury. Both Manoel and his sister noticed it and the conversation was instantly changed. But later, when Joanne and Helena were in the salon waiting for the luncheon gong, Helena surprised Joanne with her outspokenness.

'Rosa dislikes you intensely – but of course you don't need me to tell you that!' Joanne made no comment and Helena added, 'How did she take it at first – the engagement, I mean?'

'I don't know—'

'Certainly you do! We all know when we're regarded with envy; we wouldn't be women if we didn't!'

Joanne had to laugh, and went on to say, though with obvious reluctance, that she *had* noticed Rosa was not too happy about the engagement.

'That's an understatement,' chuckled Helena. She had an attractive accent, but her English was perfect. 'She hates the thought of having to leave the Solar de Alvares, because she'd become confident she was here for good. Mind you,' Helena went on, becoming grave, 'Manoel's engagement to you has come as a shock to more than Rosa. Mother's gnashing her teeth at the idea of Manoel's marrying a widow.'

Joanne turned away, staring through the window to the

fountain sparkling in the sunshine. She felt a hypocrite; it was unfair to allow Helena to go on believing in the engagement. Yet what could she do? She determined to have a word with Manoel later, and ask him if Helena could be informed of the true situation.

'I realized your mother was not pleased,' she admitted, more for something to say than anything else. 'Your stepfather didn't appear to mind, though.'

'He wouldn't; he's a pet – and never did like Rosa, so he'll be delighted at the turn of events.'

'Why does Rosa live here?' Joanne asked impulsively, even while feeling she was being disloyal to Manoel. For he had made it quite clear that he desired her to be left completely in the dark about everything that in any way concerned his cousin.

'Hasn't Manoel told you?' Helena looked curiously at her, but immediately went on, 'Rosa lost her husband when she was only twenty-eight – he died suddenly of a heart attack, so his death came as a dreadful shock to Rosa. Manoel took her to live with him, and she sort of housekeeps here. She used to be very different,' Helena added with a sudden frown. 'We went to school together and she was ever so popular. Joao's death did something to her.'

'She became embittered, you mean?'

'More than that; she became a totally different person. I don't know what our uncle would think about her now,' Helena murmured reflectively, almost forgetting Joanne's presence. 'There was no one like Rosa in his eyes. He thought more about her than all the rest of us put together. It was he who suggested Rosa should make her home with Manoel, and I rather think he hoped that eventually they'd marry.'

'This uncle – he's dead now?'

Helena nodded. 'There was some mystery about Rosa's coming here,' she went on musingly, her brow puckered in concentration. 'Manoel won't tolerate being questioned, but there was a rumour that he'd made some sort of promise to Uncle Gonçalo, and until he astounded me with the information that he was engaged to you I had fully believed the promise he made was that he would one day marry Rosa.'

Had he made such a promise? wondered Joanne. But no, for if Manoel made a promise he would keep to it, no matter what the cost to him might be. Of course, he could still marry Rosa, when his engagement to Joanne was broken, but Joanne felt sure he had no such intention.

'You believe he made some sort of promise, though?'

'I'm sure of it.' Helena gazed meditatively into the fire and there was no sound in the room for a moment. 'Perhaps he promised to give her a home for life – or until she marries again.'

The summons for lunch precluded any further discussion on the subject, but Joanne thought about it for a long while, and although she hadn't the faintest idea what the promise was, she did know without any doubt at all that Manoel's engagement had in some way been necessitated by that promise.

Manoel was curt with her when she requested that his sister should be allowed into the secret.

'It's quite unnecessary,' he almost snapped when Joanne had perseveringly repeated her request. 'I prefer that everyone shall consider us to be genuinely engaged.'

'But, Manoel . . . Helena's so nice, and I feel ashamed at deceiving her.'

'I've said all I'm going to say on the matter, Joanne. Now please don't let me hear any more about it.'

Joanne left him and went upstairs, her cheeks tingling. There was no need for him to adopt that high-handed manner towards her, or speak to her as if she were a child!

Lynn was in the sitting-room, a book lying open on her lap. She smiled as Joanne came in, and moved to one side, making room on the sofa for Joanne to sit down.

'How do you feel?' Joanne eyed her anxiously, for it was plain that Lynn was not sleeping too well.'

'Much better than if I were at home, on my own,' she returned gratefully. 'You're so kind, Joanne.'

'It's Manoel you have to thank,' Joanne said quickly. 'As soon as I told him how things were with you he immediately said you must come.'

'He's nice.' A wistful expression entered Lynn's blue eyes, for not only had she given up her career in order to care for her mother, but she had broken her engagement as well. For while her mother lived marriage was not for her. 'You'll be very happy, Joanne.'

A flush rose to Joanne's cheeks. She had not stopped to think, on eagerly agreeing to Manoel's suggestion that Lynn should come here, that her own position would prove to be extremely awkward. It was not only that her engagement was a sham, but there were also the complications brought about by her deceiving Manoel. While Lynn remained in seclusion in Joanne's apartments it had not mattered, but this morning Manoel had sent Lynn an invitation to come down to dinner, and she had accepted. All day Joanne had been dwelling on the matter and wondering what course to take. Manoel had given her a definite order to say nothing to Lynn about their engagement being a sham, but Joanne was heartily sick of deceit and finally she decided to relate the whole story to her friend.

'I know I can trust you,' she said before she began. 'You won't deliberately let anything out, but you'll have to be on your guard all the time.' And then she told Lynn the whole story, watching her changing expression and her amazement when she admitted that she and Manoel were not really engaged.

'But what a coil!' Lynn exclaimed incredulously. 'What on earth did you pose as a widow for?'

'I've told you – Manoel rubbed me up the wrong way and I hadn't the patience to put him right when he assumed I'd been married.'

Lynn shook her head, looking at Joanne in disbelief.

'You're usually so sensible,' she said, examining her as if expecting to find some actual change in her appearance. 'It just isn't you, Joanne. Surely you knew you'd find yourself in an awkward position?'

'I didn't think, at the time, that I'd ever set eyes on Manoel again – what I mean is, I never thought I'd be in such close contact with him. We were to be neighbours, I knew that, but he was so arrogant and superior that I didn't think he'd even look at me.'

'And now. . . .' Lynn glanced covertly at the ring Joanne wore. 'You'd be in a bit of a mess if you were really engaged. You'd have to tell Manoel the truth then.'

'Well, we're not really engaged, so it doesn't matter.'

A prolonged silence and then, from Lynn, curiously,

'Do you wish you were, Joanne?'

That question, so unexpected, sent Joanne into a flutter and her friend's eyes flickered perceptively.

'I – I—' Joanne broke off, then shrugged her shoulders as she noted Lynn's expression. 'I like him,' she admitted, trying not to reveal her sudden dejection.

'You more than like him. What of Manoel himself? You're most attractive, you know, Joanne.'

'Thank you, Lynn,' she said a trifle bitterly. 'But Manoel would never care for me in that way.'

'Rosa – she sounds deadly. From what you say it appears they were almost engaged before you came on the scene?'

'No, I don't believe there was anything in the rumour. Rosa wanted to marry Manoel, that's fairly certain, but I don't think he ever intended marrying her.' She went on to relate what Helena had told her. And then ended by saying, 'Whatever you do, watch Rosa. She's pumped Glee, as I've said, and she might, in her clever and subtle way, try to gain some information from you.'

'I'll take care, you can depend on me for that.' Lynn paused thoughtfully. 'You know, Joanne, the best thing you can do is go to Manoel and confess the whole. Otherwise you'll become so involved you'll never extricate yourself.'

But Joanne firmly shook her head, pointing out the impossibility of making a confession.

'His mother would consider me quite mad, and as for Manoel's reaction—' She stopped, and Lynn's face broke into a smile as Joanne gave a little shudder. 'I'm not willing to take the risk, Lynn – and after all, it's quite unnecessary, because we'll be going home soon and I'll never set eyes on Manoel again.' She reflected for a moment on his bored dismissal of the subject when she made mention of her return to England. But there was no special significance in that, she decided and put it out of her mind.

Lynn was deep in thought, and after a while she looked up, agreeing with Joanne that a confession was in fact unnecessary, but commenting on Rosa's projected visit to England and the possible consequences should she learn that Joanne had never been married and that Glee was her niece and not her daughter.

'You'll be in trouble with Manoel in any case,' she went on, but Joanne was confidently shaking her head. For only that morning Rosa had received a letter from her friends in England saying that as they had had some trouble in the family it wasn't convenient for Rosa to come so early in January, but they would welcome her towards the end of the month. Joanne told Lynn of this, adding,

'By that time I'll be back in England, so if Rosa does discover the truth and tell Manoel, I shan't be here to witness his reaction.'

'Well, that's something to be thankful for.' Lynn gave a little laugh and shook her head. 'You're a goose, Joanne. Where did you get that stubborn trait that's caused you so much trouble?'

'From my father – so Mother always asserted,' replied Joanne ruefully.

'You want to watch it in future.'

'I will,' came Joanne's swift and emphatic response. 'I'll never tell another lie as long as I live!'

'You haven't actually lied.'

'I didn't admit the truth, which is just the same.'

'Your letters,' Lynn said as the thought occurred to her. 'I sent mine to *Miss* Barrie.'

'It went to the farm, though.'

'Oh, yes, of course.'

'All my letters go there – for that reason. And I collect

121

them myself.' She turned as Glee bounced into the room, her eyes aglow.

'How long is it to Christmas now?' she asked, flopping breathlessly into a chair.

'We've had this every day since I came,' observed Lynn with an amused smile.

'Six days to Christmas Eve,' supplied Joanne. 'And tomorrow it will be five days to Christmas Eve.'

Glee chuckled, and leant back in the chair, swinging her legs.

'Why doesn't it go quicker? I can't wait!'

'You'll just have to wait.'

'Filipa and Leonor can't wait either.' She glanced at Lynn. 'Don't you want it to come quick, Auntie Lynn?'

A shadow crossed Lynn's face, but she said,

'Yes, Glee, I want it to come quickly.'

'I'm having a doll, and a bed for it, and some slippers and—'

'How do you know that?' inquired her aunt dryly.

'Those are what I've asked for.'

'Asked whom?'

'Uncle Manoel, of course. He's the one who puts the presents in the shoe.'

'In the shoe?' Lynn glanced questioningly at Joanne. 'The *shoe*?'

'It's the custom in Portugal to put your shoe on the chimneypiece on Christmas Eve and the presents are put in it.'

'What a nice idea – but, Glee, you're not going to get a doll and a bed and a pair of slippers in your shoe.'

Glee fell to contemplating her feet, still swinging vigorously to and fro.

'No, I'm not,' she agreed at length. 'That's what Filipa and Leonor said, though.'

'I expect the small presents go into the shoes,' said Joanne. And then, in a curious tone, 'Did Uncle Manoel say you were having all those things?'

Glee did not answer immediately. She was absorbed in extracting from her pocket a rather grubby paper bag in which she had a large sweet which had apparently already been in her mouth, for the paper adhered firmly to it. With difficulty she managed to remove the paper and popped the sweet into her mouth.

'No, he said I couldn't have them—' She had difficulty in talking and she pushed the sweet into her cheek, where it formed a bulge, rather like an outsize gumboil.

'Really, Glee!' Joanne exclaimed, endeavouring to appear stern. 'Where are your manners? Take that thing out of your mouth!'

'You mean spit it out?' Glee asked, shocked. 'I can't do that. Uncle Manoel said it was very rude indeed and he'd smack me next time I did it.'

'You—? You took it from your mouth in front of Uncle Manoel?'

'It was too big, and it choked me. So I had to take it out—but then I sucked it and it went smaller. Uncle Manoel said it was much too big and I mustn't buy any more. He hasn't seen these kind, so I told him it was a gob-stopper, and they're always big like this.'

'You—?' Joanne stared at her in dismay. 'You didn't say that to Uncle Manoel?'

'That it was a gob-stopper? Of course I did. That's what they're called.'

'What will he think?' Joanne turned to her friend, little realizing how comical she appeared in her dismay. 'Lynn, what will he think of her?'

'I expect he's used to kids, as he's two nieces of his own,' said Lynn unconcernedly. 'Don't look so put out; there's nothing wrong in what Glee did. So he said you couldn't have the presents you wanted?' she added, turning to Glee.

'Yes, but I know he'll get them for me.'

'How do you know that?'

'I could tell by the way he looked. But he pretended to be stern, and so I just pretended to be sad and walked away.'

The two girls glanced at one another and burst out laughing.

'That child,' prophesied Lynn when she had recovered, 'will one day twist the men round her little finger without the least effort at all.'

'Exactly what her grandmother used to say.'

'What did Gran used to say?' Glee pressed a finger to her cheek and the gumboil disappeared.

'That you're a naughty girl!'

'She didn't. She loved me. Auntie Lynn, what are you having for Christmas?'

'I don't know, Glee.'

'What do you want?'

Lynn suddenly looked very young, and very lost.

'I really don't know, Glee.'

'Ladies like scent, or powder. I bought Mummy scent last Christmas. Would you like scent?'

'That would be nice.'

'I'll tell Uncle Manoel—'

'No, Glee dear, you mustn't do that.'

'Why not? If you don't tell him he won't know what to put in your shoe.'

'You mustn't tell him I want perfume, Glee. Promise me you won't, dear?'

Glee looked at Joanne, who said she must do as Auntie Lynn told her.

'All right – but you won't get anything in your shoe,' she warned, then added, 'So it won't be any use putting your shoe on the chimneypiece, will it?'

'Glee dear,' Joanne put in swiftly, 'go and wash your face and hands. Mafalda will be taking your tea into the nursery in a few minutes. Where are Filipa and Leonor?'

'They're riding round on their bicycles. I wish I had a bicycle, then I could go with them.'

'They're not on the road?' Joanne asked quickly.

'No, just riding round the garden paths.' Glee slid off the chair and a moment later she was gone. The glasses on the sideboard rattled as she closed the door.

'Glee doesn't change one bit.' Lynn's voice held a tinge of sadness, but no regret. Her fiancé had married someone else, and had a son of two years and a five-month-old daughter. Was Lynn thinking about him now? Joanne wondered.

'Let's have some tea,' she said, rising quickly. 'I'll go myself and bring it up.'

During the next few days great activity took place at the big house on the hill, and when at last the decorations were all up it did indeed look like the fairy palace which the children chose to call it.

'They have a Christmas tree as well,' Glee said in surprise when it arrived on a cart driven by oxen. 'Do we have presents on that too?'

'You're a greedy girl,' admonished Joanne, who was on a ladder, adding a final touch of silver spray to the leaves hanging from the pelmet over the main window. The cart was outside the door and Glee ran off to join Filipa and Leonor, who were already there.

'She didn't hear you,' commented Lynn, who was also engaged in putting a few last touches to the decorations.

'She didn't want to hear,' Joanne grinned good-humouredly, and came down the ladder.

The two girls stood watching the tree being unloaded and Lynn gasped at its size.

'It's a giant!' she exclaimed, but added, 'I suppose anything smaller would look ridiculous in the hall here. I expect that's where it's going to be?'

'Yes, Lynn, it will be put in the hall.' They turned as Manoel spoke. He had entered quietly, and was standing behind them, also interested in the unloading operations. 'On the evening of Christmas Day we have a party for all the workers on the estate. It's a most happy occasion and I think you'll both enjoy it very much.' He looked at Lynn, for the coolness which had developed between him and his fiancée since the occasion of his kissing her still remained in spite of his generous act in extending this hospitality to her friend.

Lynn had instantly fallen a victim to his charms, flatly refusing to believe he could possibly have an altogether different side to his nature. And she now smiled gratefully at him, thanking him once again for inviting her to his house.

'I was feeling so dreadfully depressed,' she added, 'and this visit's changed everything. I feel different already.'

'It is not good to be alone with one's sorrow,' he returned seriously. 'One must have privacy, of course, but there should always be the knowledge that friends are close, and can be approached when the need for company is desired.'

Swallowing an unaccountable little lump in her throat, Joanne cast him a glance from under her lashes. And she could not help but be affected by the softness in his eyes and the compassionate curve of his mouth. There would always be a certain severity about him – how could it be otherwise with that haughty thrust of his chin and that dark and furrowed brow? – but the transformation effected by this inner understanding and sympathy was miraculous. For although he retained an air of rather forbidding austerity, he was at the same time incredibly handsome.

She caught her breath, watching his softened face and listening to the gravity in his voice as he spoke to her friend. Then he was telling Lynn about the party; and, as the tree was at last taken off the cart and being brought into the house he asked Lynn if she would like to help with its decoration.

'I'd love to,' was her eager response. She twisted round. 'You'll help too, Joanne?'

'Of course.'

Manoel looked down into Joanne's face; she sensed a sudden change in him, a return of the attitude of indifference he was now adopting towards her.

Why should he be like this? – just because his unnecessary over-acting annoyed her? Resentment swept over her, bringing a flush to her cheeks which in turn brought a slight lift to his arrogant brow.

'Have I done something to embarrass you?' he asked on a note of sardonic amusement, and her flush deepened.

'No, Manoel, you haven't done anything to embarrass me.'

'Then you blush for nothing,' he remarked, and gave his attention to Lynn. 'We've some new decorations, which you'll find already on the table in the hall, but we also have some from last year. Mafalda will tell you where those are.' And with that he gave a slight nod to each in turn and left them. Joanne and Lynn were in the salon, and a few minutes later his voice could be heard in the hall, where the children were excitedly watching all that went on.

'Uncle Manoel, do we have presents on the tree?'

'Certainly.'

'Will my doll be on the tree?'

'I wasn't aware you were having a doll.'

'You haven't to ask, Glee,' explained Filipa. 'Uncle Manoel knows what everyone wants.'

'How can he if you don't tell him?'

'It's magic.'

'We never tell him, but we always get what we want!' Leonor's voice was soft and husky like her mother's. 'Last Christmas I wanted seven things, and I got them all!'

'Do you come here every Christmas?' Glee wanted to know.

'We have ever since Daddy died – and for our summer holidays we go to another uncle's house, but he's got a wife because he married Mummy's sister. But they're not in Portugal at present – they're visiting our uncle's relations in America.'

'So she's your auntie,' Glee commented, and judging by the way she spoke Joanne had an awful suspicion that she was involved with one of those disgusting sweets again.

'Yes, that's right— Oh, the tree nearly toppled over! Yes, she's my auntie.'

'We've three aunties,' submitted Filipa. 'How many have you, Glee?'

'She's only got two,' Leonor put in. 'Her Auntie Chris and her Auntie Lynn.'

'So we've one more than you!'

A long pause; Joanne frowned, visualizing Glee with the sticky sweet in her fingers.

'You haven't got one more than me! I've got my Auntie Joanne.'

Lynn looked swiftly at her friend, saw Joanne's whitened cheeks and went into the hall.

'Glee, come here, I want to tell you something.'

'You haven't an Auntie Joanne!' The derisive exclamation came from Filipa, and Glee turned to Lynn for support.

'I have an Auntie Joanne, haven't I?'

Manoel had turned, puzzlement on his face as he glanced inquiringly at Lynn.

'Are you speaking of your mummy?' asked Lynn unconcernedly.

'But she's not my mummy really. She's my auntie.' Glee turned triumphantly to her friends. 'So you see, I've as many aunties as you!'

'Then you have no mummy,' Filipa said with a laugh, and Glee's face fell.

'You have to make up your mind, Glee,' said Lynn, looking at Manoel and laughing lightly. 'Glee's a romancer, Dom Manoel, I'm afraid,' she said, taking Glee's hand and making for the salon.

'What's a romancer?' inquired Glee, going meekly with Lynn.

'Darling,' said Joanne a moment later, her heart beating normally once more, 'you must choose. Do you want me for your mummy, or your aunt?'

'Can't I have both?'

'I'm afraid not.'

'Then you're my mummy,' she said – as Joanne knew she would – and gave Joanne's hand a noisy kiss.

'That was a near shave!' exclaimed Lynn when Glee had left the room once more. And she added, 'You know what? It will be a miracle if Glee doesn't eventually give you away.'

Joanne folded the ladders and picked them up.

'Then let's pray for a miracle,' she responded fervently.

'Prayers aren't always answered.'

'You sound as if you'd be glad if Glee were to give me away,' Joanne accused, frowning.

'Frankly, I don't think the result would be half so uncomfortable as you've led yourself to believe,' was Lynn's thoughtful and somewhat cryptic rejoinder.

Joanne did not pursue the subject, for it would seem that Lynn was fully convinced Manoel would accept the truth with equanimity . . . but Joanne knew otherwise.

Lynn joined them at dinner again that evening, but as usual she was very quiet, and Joanne guessed this was due as much to shyness as to her sorrow. But half-way through the meal Manoel decided to do something about it and he gave her a good deal of his attention. Lynn responded, as he intended her to, and by the time the meal was over she was much brighter than when she had sat down.

'You've been in all day?' he asked as they rose to leave the table. He glanced at her cheeks, noticing their pallor.

'I went to the village with Joanne this morning.'

Manoel turned to his fiancée.

'Would you care for a walk?' His lip curled slightly, and there was a look in his eye which conveyed the rather sardonic assurance that she would be quite safe, seeing that they would have Lynn for company.

'Yes, Manoel, that would be nice.'

Rosa was watching with narrowed eyes and, for her benefit, Manoel smiled at Joanne and said gently,

'You'll both require heavy coats; it's rather cold this evening.'

'Can I come with you?' asked Helena. 'I feel like a breath of fresh air myself.'

'Certainly.' Manoel smiled affectionately at her. 'Why ask?'

Rosa stood by the door and Joanne, feeling sorry for her, said impulsively,

'Are you coming, too, Rosa?'

'Thank you, no.' She swept from the room and went upstairs. Manoel glanced darkly at Joanne, indicating his displeasure at her inviting his cousin to accompany them on their walk.

They took to the lane this time, and although the weather had turned cooler the air was fresh and clear, with overhead an outsize moon so brilliant that the shadows it cast were as clearly defined as any silhouette picture.

'Let's take Lynn into the café in the village,' suggested Helena, and Joanne gave a little start of surprise. Not by any stretch of imagination could she see Manoel sitting in Antonio's café, drinking the local wine and listening to the music made by the mandolins and guitars of the villagers.

'Would you like that?' he inquired of Lynn, pausing on the roadside.

'Yes, very much.'

'Good, then we'll fall in with your admirable suggestion, Helena.' Catching his fiancée's surprised gaze, he opened his mouth again, as if to make some remark to her, but she swiftly glanced away, for his eyes were hard and she knew instinctively that there would be veiled sarcasm in his words. At her action Manoel changed his mind, and something in her manner touched him, for after they had walked on a few yards more she felt his arm about her shoulders.

She looked up. For whose benefit this time? Helena's, obviously ... and yet it did not seem all that necessary. A little quiver passed through her at his touch, and instantly his arm was removed. Had he misunderstood? Could it be that he believed his nearness had been distasteful to her? Impatiently Joanne shook off these thoughts. She meant no more to Manoel than did Lynn, so why should she suppose he might be interested in whether or not his touch annoyed her?

There were few people in the café, but one or two of the village girls and youths were dancing in the middle of the floor. They stopped on seeing Manoel, and so did the music. The respect with which he was regarded was evident on every face. The little scene fascinated both Lynn and Joanne, but Helena took this silent homage for granted, glancing round her and obviously expecting someone to appear and conduct them to a table. It was Antonio himself who did so, plainly honoured by the presence of the noble Dom Manoel Alvares and his companions.

Antonio spoke to Manoel in Portuguese, pulling out a chair for him as he did so.

'Yes, by all means continue with the music,' replied Manoel. 'And the dancing also.'

The café proprietor spoke again and Manoel answered in his own tongue. A bottle of the local wine was then produced, along with glasses and some light refreshments.

The music started up again, and the dancing. Joanne turned impulsively to Manoel, forgetting his coolness for the moment.

'It reminds you of all the festivity of the vintage, doesn't it?'

'The music's the same,' he reminded her. 'And the dancing.' The girls and youths were singing as they danced; Antonio was standing there, beaming and clapping his hands to the rhythm of the tambourines.

'Is this the wine they make here?' asked Lynn, tasting it.

'Yes, this is the wine we produce, Lynn. Do you like it?'

She nodded, and smiled, and Helena began telling her about the vintage.

'We make a festival here of every harvest, whatever it might be. Any gathering of crops is an excuse for a gay and social gathering. With the wine, helpers are many, and come from great distances to the *Pais do Vinho* to harvest the grapes, so of course they play their instruments and sing on the way. Then at night time they have parties at their camp.'

'And you can hear the music and singing all over the valley,' Joanne put in reflectively.

'But they work hard too,' Helena asserted. 'The treading is by no means easy.'

'They have music and singing then, I've read about it,' said Lynn. 'It helps them, because they tread to the rhythm—' She stopped, for Manoel and his sister were looking at each other and laughing. 'Have I said something wrong?'

'The music and song you mention are not really a part of the treading,' Manoel explained. 'But we oblige the tourists by laying it on especially for them.'

Lynn blinked at him. 'Only for the tourists?'

'I'm afraid so,' he smiled. 'Disappointed?'

'One always has the impression that the song and dance are a traditional part of the wine-making.'

'No.' Helena shook her head. 'Not while they're actually working.'

'There are many things laid on for the tourists,' Manoel added. 'For instance, the picturesque *rabelos* you hear about are not now used for taking the wine down the river.'

'No, I noticed that,' put in Joanne. 'I was terribly disappointed to learn that just a few are put on the river during the tourist season.'

'It's not economical to use river traffic nowadays.' Manoel filled Joanne's glass and then Helena's. 'Come, Lynn, you're not drinking.'

She was watching the dancers, but she drank up and Manoel poured her out some more wine.

An almost imperceptible lift of his finger brought Antonio to his side. Manoel spoke to him in Portuguese and within seconds an earthenware flagon appeared on the table. It was the *Vinho Verde*, product of the Minho, and Joanne said it tasted like champagne.

'It prickles your mouth,' Lynn said with a grimace.

'Not to compare with what we produce in the *Pais do Vinho*,' declared Helena loyally. 'Nothing to excel our port.'

'That's a matter of opinion,' her brother argued reasonably. 'The two wines are totally different. As you very well know, each district has its own particular wine and you can't make a comparison, for each has some quality lacking in the other. For myself, there's no drink to beat this in hot weather. It's about the most refreshing wine I've ever tasted.'

'Hmm. . . .' Helena paused after tasting the wine, holding her glass aloft and looking into it. 'You might be right, Manoel. It could be a most refreshing drink. But as Lynn says, it does prickle your tongue.'

Manoel glanced away from her, and let his eyes rest on Joanne's face. He seemed for a moment to be examining her closely, and taking in the delicately moulded features and the rare beauty of her large, widely-spaced eyes that were so like Glee's. A faint peach-like blush brought the high cheek-bones into prominence, and the soft quiver of her lips made them decidedly tempting. A muscle moved in Manoel's strong brown throat and his voice was gentle as he said,

'Come, Joanne, let us have something from you.'

She laughed, and agreed with Lynn and Helena that the *Vinho Verde* prickled the tongue.

'I definitely like our wine better.' She hadn't noticed what she said until her fiancé's brow lifted quizzically and the pale flush deepened to an enchanting rosy glow.

'Our wine?'

'Perhaps I should have said your wine.'

His amusement grew; he laughed and said,

'I liked your first answer, my dear,' and then he added, 'In any case, mine is not the only *quinta* in the Douro!'

A vision of the valley came before her eyes; the dressers working on the terraces of schist – cutting, spraying and giving all their energies to the vines. She saw the pretty red and white *quintas*, with their verandahs and gardens and tiled roofs overshadowed by cypress trees. These enchanting villas were the homes of the wealthy wine-growers of the *Pais do Vinho* – the Country of the Wine.

'All right then – our wine; the wine of the Douro.' Joanne was looking at Manoel, but at a movement behind him she shifted her gaze . . . and embarrassment flooded over her as she saw Ricardo about to sit down at the table by the door. Manoel turned in order to see what had caused her confusion. Joanne had introduced Ricardo to Manoel on the evening Ricardo had visited her, the evening she had discovered the depth of her feelings for Manoel, and told Ricardo of that discovery. As Ricardo was going Manoel had come from his study and the two men had met. Manoel now turned again; his glance fell on Joanne for a second and his attitude was one of indecision. But almost at once he said,

'Your friend's alone, Joanne. Would you have him join us?'

'I . . .' Her embarrassment grew, for the only thing she could remember was her admission, and Ricardo's absolute refusal to believe it was true. At last however she managed to convince him and he had gone away looking so glum and downcast that Joanne had felt utterly miserable and weighed down by guilt.

'Yes – yes,' she stammered as Manoel watched in some puzzlement for her answer.

Manoel invited Ricardo to come to their table, which he did, though not with any apparent enthusiasm. However, once the introductions were over he appeared more at ease and Joanne was rather pleasantly surprised at the way Manoel spoke to him – aloofly, it was true, but that was his way with all but his intimates. His manner, though was decidedly friendly and after a little while Joanne thought it was nice to have another man in the company. It evened things out a little.

Several times during the next half hour Joanne noticed Ricardo's glance straying to Lynn; he seemed interested in her, and Joanne put this down to the fact that although she joined in the conversation, and laughed when humour was appropriate, there was a sadness about her which, quite understandably, she could not hide.

When at last Manoel said it was time to go he surprised everyone by inviting Ricardo to the party on the evening of Christmas Day.

'But I don't work on the estate,' Ricardo said, thinking Manoel had probably overlooked that circumstance.

'Your father did. Perhaps your mother would like to come also?'

Ricardo made some mention of his mother, Joanne recalled. Manoel must have remembered what Ricardo said, and he now invited her because she would be left on her own if Ricardo came without her.

'Mother would thoroughly enjoy it, I'm sure.' Ricardo's eyes brightened eagerly. 'Yes, Dom Manoel, we'll accept your invitation – and thank you very much indeed.'

'That's all right. Your mother doesn't get out much, I think you said?'

'Not since Father died. She always says she feels uncomfortable if she goes out on her own.'

'How, then, does she pass her time?'

'She has the housework – and she loves to embroider.'

'Embroider? You mean on canvas?' he inquired, and Joanne's wide brow puckered in surprise. Lynn, too, looked faintly puzzled at this interest shown in Ricardo's mother, but Helena regarded her brother with only the merest trace of curiosity. It was almost as if she were used to his making inquiries such as this.

'No,' answered Ricardo ruefully. 'She embroiders on silk, using silks, and makes the most beautiful pictures. But the materials she uses are so expensive that she can't do as much as she likes.'

'That's a pity . . . a great pity.' The subject was dropped, and after they had stood at the door of the café just long enough to say good night, Manoel and the three girls took the uphill lane and Ricardo went off in the opposite direction.

Immediately they reached the Solar de Alvares Joanne and Lynn bade Manoel and his sister good night and went up to Joanne's own apartments. Some sort of reaction took possession of Lynn and she looked ready to burst into tears.

Watching her, Joanne felt quite full up, but knew that nothing she could do or say would help. Lynn was thinking of her mother, and Joanne was reluctant to offer sympathy for fear of making her feel worse. But when Lynn was in bed Joanne went downstairs again to Manoel.

'That drink you gave me, to make me sleep,' she said. 'Can I have some for Lynn?'

'She's not well?' he asked in swift concern.

'It's nothing except depression; she's dwelling on things. I feel she ought to be given something to make her sleep.'

'Quite right.'

Five minutes later Joanne was standing by Lynn's bed, waiting for Lynn to drain the glass.

'You'll be asleep in no time at all,' she assured her. 'And you'll feel much better tomorrow.'

'Thanks, Joanne, you and Manoel are so good to me. I'm so grateful – but I can't say anything that seems adequate.'

'Nonsense; you haven't to be grateful. Manoel says we're here to help one another, and that's absolutely true. Lie down now and I'll fix the bedclothes.'

Lynn snuggled down in the bed and looked up at Joanne.

'Ricardo's nice – and so good-looking.'

'I think so too. He—'

'Yes?' Lynn waited, puzzled by her friend's hesitation. 'What were you going to say?'

That he wanted to marry her. . . . That was what she had been going to say – but for some quite incomprehensible reason she had bitten back the words even as they were on the tip of her tongue.

'Nothing important,' returned Joanne carelessly. 'Now, there's the sheet tucked in, and the blanket. Are you quite warm and comfortable?'

'Lovely and warm – and comfortable.' She was drowsy, within minutes her eyes were closed and her breathing became regular. Her face was relaxed, serene. Yes, thought Joanne with satisfaction, the sleeping draught was just what she needed.

CHAPTER EIGHT

CHRISTMAS EVE in the home of any Portuguese *fidalo* was the scene of much gaiety and song, and the Solar de Alvares was no exception. The long table held a glittering array of silver, from the ornate candelabra to the pretty little flower-holders containing individual posies at each place setting. All Dom Manoel's family and friends were gathered for the traditional supper of *pacalhau*, after which there was to be folk-dancing by a group of girls and youths in their colourful national costumes.

As Joanne was presented to the various members of her fiancé's family she could not help wondering how he was to break the engagement without much loss of face. But the matter seemed not to trouble him at all, and his whole demeanour, though edged with his customary reserve, was to all outward appearances that of the proud and happy lover.

'We're most delighted to meet you.' Nuno Alvares had all his brother's cool assurance and haughty air, but he also possessed the ability to unbend when the occasion demanded it. His wife, small and pretty, had a vivacious personality which instantly put Joanne at her ease.

'How surprised we all were!' she exclaimed, taking Joanne's arm and propelling her to the sofa by the window. They were in the salon, awaiting the call to supper. 'Tell me all about it; I'm simply dying to know how it's happened. I still can't believe Manoel's fallen in love at last. You came to Portugal to farm Pendela, he tells me?'

'Yes, that's right.' At the rueful note in her voice Isobella nodded understandingly.

'It was in a dreadful state. Dona Amelia neglected it shockingly, but she was very old and infirm at the end. She ought to have sold out to Manoel long ago' – Isobella broke off, then laughed. 'That wasn't quite the right thing to say, was it? Had Dona Amelia sold the farm to Manoel, then he'd never have met you.'

If, like her sister-in-law, Isobella had any preconceived ideas about Manoel and his cousin she tactfully refrained from mentioning them. But she did go on to say that Manoel's choice had come as a shock to his mother. 'I think your being a widow, with a child, quite upset her, but she'll recover. She didn't care for me at first, but she now seems to have made the best of it.'

'You weren't good enough for Nuno, you mean?'

'No position – or fortune,' returned Isobella with a sort of grim humour.

'Then it's no wonder she doesn't approve of me ...' Joanne tailed off and, concluding the reason to be embarrassment at Joanne's apparent lack of diplomacy Isobella said with a laugh,

'Don't let it trouble you; her opinion counts for nothing with any of her children. As for Manoel, when he makes up his mind a dozen Dona Clementinas wouldn't change it.' She chatted on, plainly delighted with her prospective sister-in-law. Becoming too uncomfortable to speak, Joanne sat silently gazing over to where Dona Clementina was reclining on the couch, engaged in conversation with Rosa. On occasions one or the other would cast a glance in Joanne's direction, and it was plain that she was the object of their discussion. What were they saying about her? Joanne wondered, but soon lost interest, as her attention had been caught by Senhor Pedro, who was talking to Lynn. They were at the far end of the room; both were smiling and Joanne noticed with extreme satisfaction that Lynn looked far brighter than when she had first arrived at the Solar de Alvares.

Following the direction of her gaze, Isobella turned the conversation to Lynn.

'Manoel was saying that Lynn has recently lost her mother.'

'Just over a fortnight ago. They were devoted, and Lynn's feeling pretty bad at present.' A pause, and then Joanne added impulsively, 'I thought it was wonderful of Manoel to let her come here. Just imagine how she'd have felt – being all alone at Christmas.'

'It would have been grim – but of course Manoel would think of that immediately you told him about her.' She spoke matter-of-factly and it was clear that she saw nothing exceptional in her brother-in-law's action. 'He has the extraordinary faculty of seeing everything at a glance. And, having done so, he then wastes no time at all in doing something about it.'

How true! Joanne reflected on the way he had arranged everything on the occasion of Glee's accident. Within minutes he had had it all organized, right down to the last detail.

'It's doing her the world of good,' Joanne observed, glancing again at her friend. 'She appears to be getting along fine with Senhor Pedro.'

'Everyone gets along with Pedro – even his wife,' Isobella added with a grimace. 'It was a happy day when he became one of the family.'

What had attracted him to the formidable Dona Clementina? On the surface it would seem they had nothing in common, but perhaps, like her son, Dona Clementina had a different side to her nature. Manoel was approaching Joanne and her companion, striding down the length of the salon, a truly majestic figure, poised and faultlessly dressed. A slight nod now and then to someone as he passed added to the impression of magnificence, and Joanne caught her breath as he came nearer. Isobella said, as if actually sensing her little inaudible gasp,

'Was ever any man so handsome as my brother-in-law? I believed Nuno would be the handsomest man I'd ever meet . . . but then he introduced me to Manoel!'

'May I join you?' Manoel requested, smiling. 'Or is the subject matter for feminine ears only?'

'I was talking about you, Manoel.' Isobella gave him an affectionate glance. 'But I'll definitely not tell you what I was saying.'

'You won't be pressed, then.' Although his voice held a sort of bored disinterest his eyes still smiled. 'Joanne dear, I see that your friend is a little happier tonight.'

'It's the influence of Pedro,' declared Isobella, flicking a glance in their direction. She rose then, saying she had better go and have a few words with Dona Lucia Casco, her aged aunt. 'Otherwise I shall come under the lash of that dreadful tongue of hers,' she added with a grimace, 'and you haven't the least idea of how uncomfortable that can be, Manoel.'

His brows lifted a fraction.

'I'm not lacking imagination,' he retorted, though with a trace of amusement in his voice. 'Soften her up, Isobella, for it will be my duty to sit with her later on.'

'Is she so frightening?' Joanne asked, becoming awkward now that she and Manoel were alone.

'She's most certainly an irascible old lady,' he said. 'But she suffers greatly from rheumatism, so perhaps we should make allowances.' Turning to Joanne, he changed the subject. 'I'm completely in the dark as to this coldness you've adopted with me, Joanne, but I must ask you to oblige me – for tonight while my guests are here – by acting as a fiancée should.'

She forgot her awkwardness as she started in surprise. As Manoel had made no previous mention of it she had assumed him to be resigned to her change of manner, and it amazed her that he could sink his pride and request a favour such as this from her.

Eyes were naturally upon them, as they sat there on the sofa, close together, with Manoel smiling affectionately at her, so she had to repress the militant sparkle that would have leapt to her eyes, and she even managed to smile as she said,

'It isn't possible. You see, the situation's artificial and I'm always conscious of the fact.' And then it was that Joanne realized it was no request, made humbly, but a definite order which her fiancé meant to have obeyed. For although the only indication of his anger was an almost imperceptible tightening of his mouth, it was quite sufficient to bring a tingle of apprehension to her spine; the softly uttered words which followed crushed any further resistance she might have been contemplating.

'You'll do as I say, Joanne – or answer to me.' And as Diego then appeared to announce supper was ready no more was said on the matter.

But, strangely, after the first flash of resentment at his peremptory laying down of the law, Joanne experienced no ill feeling against him, and all through the meal she was able to respond to his attentions and smiles without the slightest difficulty or strain. And she even managed to call him darling on one occasion ... surprising herself equally as much as she surprised Manoel.

Immediately after supper the dancers arrived, and the musicians, who were just as colourfully arrayed as the girls and youths from the village. The great hall was brought into use and after a while the floor was the scene of even greater activity as the guests themselves joined in the dance.

'Come, my love.' Taking her hand, Manoel pulled Joanne into the ring. A protest arose to her lips, for she was afraid she might look foolish, but he ignored her hesitancy, adding, 'You did very well the last time, so there's nothing to worry about.'

As on the previous occasion Joanne thoroughly enjoyed the dancing, and when it was all over and the guests had departed she flopped into a chair, tired but unaccountably happy. Lynn stayed only a moment or two and then said good night, leaving Joanne and Manoel alone in the salon. The lights had earlier been extinguished, for everyone was in the hall, and the only illumination came from a branch of candles standing on the mantelpiece.

Manoel stood by it, his face in the shadows cast by the softly flickering light. On the mantelpiece were the children's shoes, which they had been allowed to place there before going to bed. Rosa's shoe was there, and Helena's, as also were those of Manoel's mother and stepfather, for they were staying at the Solar de Alvares for the Christmas celebrations. Joanne's and Lynn's shoes were missing.

'Don't you put out your shoe?' asked Joanne, looking rather shyly at him. There was the merest hesitation and then Manoel said yes, he did put out his shoe. If he noticed the slight clearing of her brow he chose to ignore it as he added,

'I see that Lynn has forgotten hers.'

'I think she was reluctant because it would seem like asking for a present,' Joanne submitted, and his brow contracted in a frown.

'It would have been no such thing; our custom is for everyone in the house to place their shoe on the chimneypiece. Decidedly she must put it out.'

'She won't be in bed yet. Shall I go and tell her?'

'Diego will do it,' he said, and jerked the bell rope. His butler emerged from the darkness around them. 'Tell Senhora Lynn to bring down her shoe – No, she's probably tired. Bring it down yourself.' He glanced at Joanne. 'If what you say is true she would be embarrassed at having to come in here with it.'

For a moment Joanne said nothing, merely shaking her head as she looked up at him, wonderment and admiration shining in her eyes.

'You're so understanding, and . . . kind,' she murmured at last.

His eyes flickered strangely.

'You didn't think so once,' he remarked with some amusement, and then, because she seemed to be enveloped in confusion at his words, he added prosaically, 'Have you enjoyed your first Christmas Eve in Portugal?' He moved to occupy the place beside her on the couch and continued, before she could frame a reply to his question, 'You looked very lovely, Joanne. I was exceedingly proud of you.' Emotion brought colour to her delicate features and Manoel's lips parted in a smile. 'You look even lovelier now.'

Flattery such as this was unnecessary, so why did he indulge in it? But the nature of his smile was such that she was forced to respond. The night had been gay; she had been admired and toasted, and the happiness resulting from her fiancé's attention was still with her.

'Thank you, Manoel,' she returned, apparently absorbed in a contemplation of the last dying embers of wood ash in the grate.

'You haven't answered my question.'

Her *first* Christmas Eve in Portugal. . . . An odd way of putting it, but there was no special significance, she told herself.

'I've had the most wonderful evening of my life,' she admitted truthfully. 'I enjoyed every minute of it.'

'Perhaps you'll enjoy tomorrow night even more. You will help me give out the presents, of course.' The great tree was loaded with gifts, most of which were for the *quinta* employees and their children.

'I—? But won't Helena or Rosa expect to do that?'

'Not now. You're the one who'll be expected to assist me.' His dark glance flicked over her, still with admiration. 'It won't be any trouble to you, I hope?'

'I'll thoroughly enjoy it!' she exclaimed impulsively. But a tiny sigh followed her words. If only she were really going to marry him! It seemed inconceivable that she wanted to do so, considering she had disliked him so intensely at the start.

'What was that for, Joanne?' he asked seriously. 'You've appeared to be so happy, and now we have a sigh. Tell me the reason for it?'

Joanne sought for words, for his voice was a command, but to her relief Diego entered, with Lynn's shoe in his hand.

'The *senhora*'s shoe,' he said quietly, and placed it on the chimneypiece. 'Will there be anything else, Dom Manoel?'

'Nothing, thank you, Diego. Good night.'

'How is it that all your servants speak English?' Joanne wanted to know, eyeing him curiously.

'Some instruction is given in school. Also, it's surprising

how quickly one can pick up enough to make oneself understood.'

'I'm certainly not picking up Portuguese very quickly,' she confessed. 'It must be the fastest spoken language in the world, for I find it quite impossible to catch even the odd word.'

'You'll grasp it in time,' was his surprising response, and a frown touched her brow. She spoke her thoughts aloud, saying,

'I don't understand you, Manoel. I – I shan't be here long enough to learn the language.'

'No?' He leant back against the cushions, from where he regarded her with an expression she had never seen before. 'Why the hesitation?' he inquired softly.

'It—' She spread her hands. 'It wasn't intentional.'

'You're looking forward to going home?'

She gazed into the fire, disturbed by his question. Once she left here she would be most unlikely ever to set eyes on Manoel again. The thought dismayed her, and yet she knew that the sooner she left Portugal the better it would be for her. Relieved of the torture, she could expect her wounds to heal, though how long it would be before she could think of Manoel without this tug of pain at her heart she did not know. Forgetting would be a long and difficult process and she wished fervently she had never come to Portugal – but this time her wish was far removed from any financial losses incurred by her stubborn refusal of his most generous offer. A little intake of his breath gave hint of his impatience for her answer and she replied truthfully,

'I shall be glad to go home, Manoel.'

Joanne could not have said what she expected. Bored disinterest, perhaps; a mention of payment for her land. . . . But instead she saw a return of that new expression of a moment or two ago, an expression so hard and unyielding that she wondered what could possibly be running through his mind. She was not left long in suspense.

'Unfortunately my plans have gone awry. At the time, I considered it would be enough for us to become engaged. It is now necessary that we marry.'

She stared at him. Her lips parted, but no words came. It seemed impossible that he could sit there so calmly, his only emotion one of determination, which was clearly portrayed in that hard expression with which he still regarded her.

'You said – you said your plans would materialize when – when the children left,' she managed to stammer at length. 'The children haven't gone yet.'

'They'll be leaving here in less than a week. I have every indication that their going won't after all relieve my position.' Relieve? What an odd word to use, Joanne thought, as Manoel paused as if choosing his words carefully. 'Marriage is the only solution. And from your point of view it will be most beneficial, for you can't continue like this all your life, struggling to bring up Glee on your own.' He smiled then, and the hardness left his face. 'Don't look at me with such consternation, child! I'm not an ogre. You're perfectly comfortable here at present?'

Joanne nodded bewilderedly, her mind in chaos. Manoel had just proposed to her – or rather, told her she must marry him! There was nothing in the world she desired more than to become his wife, and yet she was trying desperately to frame the words of a refusal!

'I'm c-comfortable, yes, but—'

'And you like Portugal?'

'Oh, yes – I love it—'

'Glee does, too, and has made some little friends. She's quite popular at school, I hear. Filipa and Leonor, too – they come here often, and during the holidays Glee would be able to stay with them for a change.' He stood up, ostensibly to stir the embers into a glow, but he remained on his feet, looking down at her, and she was forced to tilt her head right back in order to meet his gaze. 'I'm fully aware that you don't love me, Joanne, but as I don't love you either it isn't important. I suggest we arrange an early date for the wedding; there's nothing to wait for, and the sooner we're married the sooner my plan will succeed.'

'I can't marry you!' she blurted out, quite unable to find

145

any more fitting way of saying it. 'The whole idea's ridiculous!' But she was almost in tears, and her voice was high-pitched and cracked. For at his casual dismissing of the vital matter of love a knife had turned in her heart.

'Ridiculous?' he echoed, his brow lifting in surprised interrogation. 'Why?'

'We – we can't marry without love.'

'It wouldn't be the first time a couple have married without love. No, Joanne, it's not ridiculous. On the contrary, it's a most sensible course for us to take. We shall both benefit greatly by it.'

She shook her head, noting his frown at her action. But he did not know all. . . . How would he react, she wondered, were she to tell him the real reason for her hesitancy? Hesitancy. . . . Joanne gave a visible start of surprise on suddenly realizing that her thoughts lacked consistency – that her swiftly uttered exclamation was definitely half-hearted!

'We'd never make a success of it,' she murmured at last, rather feebly.

'Certainly it will be a success.' He passed that off as of no importance whatever. But then he made a pronouncement that swept away all her indecision, submerging every other emotion except the profound desire to become his wife. 'Who knows, Joanne, one day – quite unexpectedly – love might enter into our relationship.' The odd inflection in his voice, and the manner with which he looked at her, seemed at variance with his former casual assertion that there existed no love between them. It would almost seem that he did in fact already have some slight affection for her – Joanne pulled herself up. What impossible notion was this? Her thoughts were so chaotic that they were shooting off in all directions.

'I don't know what to say,' she quivered, on the point of capitulation.

Manoel sat down, and took her hand in his. Her fingers were icy cold and he used his other hand caressingly, imparting to her some of its warmth.

'You're tired, my dear. Go to bed; and tomorrow you'll be

able to think more clearly. Then we can talk, and fix the date for our wedding.'

She turned to him, her lovely grey eyes wide and searching.

'I haven't said yes, Manoel,' she faltered, rather like a frightened child.

Her expression was not lost on him and he said, rather gently,

'You don't trust me to be good to you? Ah, but you must, Joanne. There's absolutely nothing for you to fear.' And as if to strengthen his words – and perhaps expel that last faint trace of resistance, he placed a gentle kiss upon her cheek.

A few minutes later, after they had been sitting there, Manoel apparently absorbed in nothing more important than the last flickering gleam from the dying embers, and Joanne wondering how long she could put off the evil moment of revelation, Manoel told her to go up and fetch her shoe.

'Or use one of those,' he added, glancing down at her feet. She took off her silver slippers and, rising, placed one on the mantelpiece. And then she turned. Manoel sat there, looking quite good-humoured and accessible. Should she tell him now – take advantage of this opportune moment to get the whole thing off her mind? She actually opened her mouth and then her courage failed her. Better to leave it until after Christmas, she decided, and finding no valid reason for doing so – reluctantly admitted to being a shirker.

She bade him good night and went out, taking her other shoe with her, and making no sound as she crossed the hall to the corridor at the other end from where the staircase rose in an ornate ironwork spiral to the upper floor of the house. The library door was ajar and from within came the sound of voices – Dona Clementina's raised, and that of her husband soft and mildly tolerant. So they hadn't yet gone to bed. About to pass on, Joanne heard her name mentioned, and although the two spoke in their own language she instinctively stopped. Dona Clementina was speaking, her tones as haughty and cold as ever. Her husband replied in English.

'You mean Rosa's not going?'

'Why should she? Manoel promised, and he must abide by it!' Dona Clementina now spoke in English.

'He didn't promise to give Rosa a home for ever.'

'He promised his uncle he'd never turn Rosa out of the Solar de Alvares.'

'But now he's engaged he'll expect her to leave of her own accord.'

'It's her home; has been ever since Manoel made the promise.'

'I should imagine, my dear,' commented Senhor Pedro after a pause, 'that your son made the greatest— No, the only mistake of his life, probably, when he gave his uncle that promise.' And he added, 'When they're married, then, is Rosa going to have the nerve to stay on in their home?'

'*Manoel's* home, if you please, Pedro! Naturally if Manoel were married to this girl, Rosa would have no alternative but to leave. But it so happens that there isn't going to be a marriage.'

Joanne's eyes opened wide. She could not have moved now even though she was well aware that she had no right to listen.

'I see. . . . I wondered what you were talking about when you had your heads together this evening – and looking across at Joanne, who must have known she was being discussed.'

'Who cares?' A small pause and then Dona Clementina inquired curiously, 'When did *you* reach the conclusion that there wasn't to be a wedding?'

'I didn't, but the idea kept on troubling me. You believe Manoel got engaged for the specific purpose of forcing Rosa to leave his house?'

'I do. For some obscure reason he's turned against Rosa—'

'If you'll excuse me, my dear,' interrupted her husband mildly, 'the reason is far from obscure. Rosa just isn't nice to know, and in my opinion Manoel's been a hero to tolerate her all this time, for not only does she interfere in his life and his business, but she never allows him to forget the fact that their uncle hoped one day they would marry.'

'And so they ought to do! As for Rosa's not being nice – she's a charming girl – with the manners, the breeding and the fortune which my son desires in a wife. This other girl has nothing!'

'Except her beauty. It might in time turn even Manoel's head.'

'He'll never marry the girl, never! This engagement's merely a conspiracy between them. He's probably bribed her with some stupidly high offer for her farm, and so she agreed to help him. Manoel fully expected Rosa would decide to leave when the children went home to Helena, and if you were to question that girl, and she told you the truth, you'd discover that the engagement's to last for only another week.'

'Does Manoel know yet that Rosa isn't leaving?'

'He knows, because she was talking earlier on about inviting these English friends over for their summer holiday. She said Manoel looked dumbfounded, but made no comment about it.'

'So Manoel is fully aware that his plan has failed?'

'Certainly.'

'And you honestly believe – knowing your son as you do – that he'll allow Rosa to get the better of him in this way?'

'What can he do about it?'

A long silence. Joanne's heart missed a beat as she heard the door of the salon open.

'What can he do? Go all the way and marry the girl! That'll move Rosa quickly enough,' were the last words Joanne heard as she sped towards the stairs.

She lay awake a long while, going over what she had heard. Everything was explained. Having made the promise, Manoel would never break it. But, with Rosa's attitude becoming intolerable, and, therefore, her presence more and more irksome, he had decided to put her in a position where she would quit his house of her own accord. At first, Rosa had formed the opinion that there was some mystery about Joanne, and that she was not free to marry. Eventually she appeared to become resigned, although she had made subtle insinuations that she might make some inquiries whilst in England. Now, however, she had guessed the truth – or, more probably, it was Dona Clementina who had hit upon the idea that her son had taken measures to rid himself of Rosa's presence.

Joanne yawned and became drowsy. Would she have agreed to marry Manoel had she overheard the conversation earlier? Yes, most decidedly, for although she knew it was far from commendable, she experienced some considerable satisfaction at the prospect of both Rosa's and Dona Clementina's consternation when eventually they should learn that there was to be a wedding after all.

She was up very early the following morning, and so was Lynn, for they had both bought presents for Manoel. Joanne's was a leather-bound book of poems and Lynn's was a key-ring, attached to which was a beautiful little model of St. Christopher, hand-carved in ivory.

'Mine will go in, but what about yours?' Lynn asked, putting her attractive little parcel into the shoe.

'It'll have to go on top. See, most of the others are on top.'

Manoel had put all the presents out, and Joanne wondered who had tied them up, for they were all prettily wrapped and secured with coloured ribbons.

'We'd better go,' she said, cocking an ear. 'I do believe those children are coming downstairs.'

She and Lynn reached the sitting-room before any of the children appeared, and Joanne made some coffee, using the electric kettle which Manoel had provided.

They sat quietly for a while and then Joanne decided to relate to Lynn all that had happened last night.

'You're going to marry Dom Manoel?' Lynn gasped, and immediately added, a trifle anxiously, 'But if he's doing it just to get rid of Rosa, how can—? What I mean is, will you be happy, Joanne . . . without love?'

'I love him,' she admitted. 'But you've already guessed that.'

'Yes— Manoel, though, if he doesn't care for you it's going to be – well, difficult, to say the least.'

Joanne sipped her coffee, her eyes pensive yet strangely shining with hope. For hadn't Manoel said himself that one day love might enter into their relationship? Prospects for their future could not be so bad if he were able to say a thing like that. And her own love was strong; surely she could convey this to him without suffering too great an embarrassment.

'I'm quite optimistic,' she said at length. 'My only dread now is that of telling Manoel I'm not a widow. Everyone is going to think I'm completely mad for adopting a pose like that.'

'It's certainly going to be awkward,' agreed Lynn ruefully. 'I know I advised you to own up, but on thinking it over I must admit you're not in a very enviable position.'

'And it gets worse.' Joanne gave a little deprecating laugh. 'It didn't matter when we were only going to be engaged, but now the truth will have to come out.' She frowned at the idea of her fiancé's anger – for angry he would be at having to explain to his relatives and friends. 'I wish I had the courage to get it over and done with, but I've decided to wait until after Christmas.'

'For what reason?'

'I really haven't the faintest idea. One instinctively puts off some unpleasant task until the last possible moment.'

'And suffers the added anxiety. If you're going to do it – and of course you have no alternative – then do it now.'

But Joanne shook her head. She was not going to spoil her Christmas for anything.

And it did in fact prove to be a memorable time for both Joanne and Lynn. Everyone came down and received their gifts, and then gave presents to each other. Manoel smiled affectionately at Joanne as he opened his book, and a moment after thanking her he was thanking Lynn for her charming little gift. For Lynn there was an expensive perfume, and she whisperingly inquired of Joanne how Manoel could have known she liked this particular one.

'He asked me,' was the simple explanation.

Joanne's present from Manoel took her breath away. It was a bracelet in twisted cords of gold, with a clasp of diamonds and rubies. She took it from its bed of velvet and for a moment could only stare at it, the tears hanging on her lashes.

'Oh, Joanne, how lovely!' The involuntary exclamation came from Lynn, who was at her side. She fingered it and told Joanne to put it on. 'Shall I fasten it for you?'

'Y-yes, please.' Joanne looked up at Manoel, and blinked back the tears.

'Thank you,' she said simply, too full to add anything more.

Manoel said nothing, for which Joanne was grateful, and after a little while she regained her composure and was able to take an interest in Leonor and Filipa, who were excitedly showing her their presents. All Glee had in her shoe was a tiny doll in a bed no bigger than a matchbox. She stared unbelievingly, then thanked Manoel quietly, her lip trembling. But the next moment she was clapping her hands as Manoel indicated a large bag lying on the hearth. In it was everything she had asked for, although Manoel told her with mock sternness that she didn't deserve them because she had asked.

'And now come and see what you get when you don't ask,' he invited, taking her hand. Over in the corner, behind the sofa, was a shining bicycle in blue and chrome.

'Oh . . .!' breathed Glee, staring at it. 'Uncle Manoel, I didn't think you would know I wanted a bike!'

'She's going to cry!' exclaimed Filipa unbelievingly, but Joanne felt she herself would cry any moment now.

'Manoel,' she said huskily, 'you're so good.'

'Nonsense, Joanne. Glee felt left out, with Filipa and Leonor having bicycles. They leave them here, so she will be able to ride with them whenever they come to stay.' He lifted it out and held it while Glee sat on it.

Rosa and Dona Clementina were looking at one another, and Joanne made an effort to blink back the tears as she thanked Manoel for his gift to Glee.

'It's such an expensive one,' she added. 'Glee, you must take good care of it.'

'I didn't think you would know I wanted a bike so much,' Glee said again. She was still sitting on the saddle, but she twisted right round and, reaching up, put both arms round Manoel's neck and kissed him loudly. 'I love you very much,' she said, and pushed a knuckle into her eyes.

'Well, both you and your mother are the oddest creatures,' he said with a laugh, relieving the tension. 'I don't know that I'll buy either of you a present next year—' He broke off as Joanne started visibly at his words. 'Come,' he said briskly to Glee, 'off you get.'

'Can't I ride it now?'

'After breakfast. Leonor and Filipa will go with you.'

The real highlight of Christmas was not the magnificent lunch that was served instead of dinner, but the party in the evening for the workers on the estate, and their children. A long table had been placed in the salon and it was literally loaded with food. The adults helped themselves, but the servants looked after the children. Then there was dancing and games, with prizes for the winners. Finally the presents were taken from the tree. Every single one had a name upon it and had been chosen with care. In previous years Rosa had assisted Manoel with the handing out of the gifts, and she stood at one side, an ugly expression on her face as she watched Joanne taking the presents from Manoel as he cut them from the tree. Ricardo received initialled handkerchiefs and his mother embroidery silks. As Joanne handed the be-ribboned cellophane box to the beaming Senhora Lopes she recalled Manoel's interest in her hobby ... and wondered how long it would be before she really knew this man whom she was so soon to marry.

Senhora Lopes had been enjoying herself just sitting there, watching the various activities and chatting to neighbours, and during the evening Joanne's eyes had repeatedly strayed to Ricardo and Lynn. They danced together, had their refreshments over in a corner by themselves, and they now stood by the window, Ricardo's hand on Lynn's shoulder as they watched Manoel and Joanne with the presents. So intently was she absorbed in them that Joanne failed to take the present Manoel was handing to her, and, stooping down, he whispered in her ear,

'Yes, it is interesting, my dear, but you have work to do.'

She laughed then, and turned her face up; her action was swift and her cheek touched his chin. She blushed adorably and said in some haste,

'Oh, Manoel, do you think . . . ?'

'It's early to say, but I have a feeling that Lynn isn't going to be in any hurry to leave us. A present for Senhora Mendonça,' he added briskly, handing the parcel to Joanne. 'And one for her husband.'

When all the presents had been given out and everyone was ready to leave, a young man from the village, one of Manoel's most conscientious employees, asked that he round off the party with a ballad he had written on hearing of the engagement. As he spoke in Portuguese Joanne could not understand a word, and Manoel had to explain. Ricardo was also explaining to Lynn.

Manoel then nodded to the young man, who sat down on a chair and began playing his guitar.

'The music is a Coimbra *fado* – quite well-known,' Manoel said. 'But Tomás has put some words to it especially for us. He calls it the *Fado of Joanne and Manoel*.'

Everyone stopped talking and the music of the guitar and the clear deep voice of Tomás echoed through the great high-ceilinged hall. Manoel sat down on the dais on which the tree stood, drawing Joanne down with him and retaining her hand.

'He sings that all are delighted with the betrothal . . . we are wished much happiness and long life. . . .' Manoel paused to listen and then continued in a whisper, his lips close to her ear, 'It's the wish of everyone that we have an heir with his father's virtues and his mother's beauty— I don't know about the former,' he added with a soft laugh, 'but there's no doubt at all about the latter.' His lips touched her hair, and his cool breath caressed her cheek. Emotion filled her and although she turned with the intention of making some remark, she stopped, for shyness overcame her. Tomás continued singing. Manoel translated for her, 'And it is the hope that we shall be blessed with many more children, and that we can always laugh together in our joys and comfort each other in our sorrows.'

The *fado* came to an end; silence filled the room for a moment and then the applause rang out, continuing until Manoel rose and lifted a hand for silence. Joanne stood up; all eyes were on her and she saw only smiles and indications of goodwill until her eyes wandered to where Rosa was sitting on a couch, where she had been for most of the evening, talking to Dona Clementina. On the older woman's face there was intense dislike; on Rosa's there was undisguised hatred. Swiftly Joanne looked away, back to the smiles and admiring glances before her. In his own tongue Manoel thanked his guests for coming and then talked for a few minutes to the children, who were sitting on the floor in a half-circle, each holding his or her parcel, and a little string bag filled with nuts and chocolates and other confections. Then he said in English,

'For the very beautiful *fado* both my fiancée and I thank you very much indeed.'

Cheers broke out; the Portuguese were the most friendly people in the world, Joanne decided, her own face flushed with pleasure. Then someone shouted in English,

'When is the wedding to be?'

Manoel glanced swiftly down at Joanne and immediately raised his head again.

'There's no definite date fixed, but the month is January.'

Joanne gave a faint start and looked up. Manoel was smiling and after a little hesitation she responded. Rosa and

Dona Clementina were gaping in disbelief and, watching her fiancé's expression as he glanced across at them, Joanne sensed his satisfaction and relief.

They were on their own later and Joanne, flushed with happiness, admitted that the evening had excelled even the previous one.

'You're going to be a great success yourself, my dear. It's very clear that you've won every heart.' He took both her hands and drew her unresistingly to him. He was so tall and dark above her, and so close . . . Joanne trembled and would have broken away, but he held her tightly in his embrace.

'Are my kisses so very distasteful to you, Joanne?' he asked, a curious inflection in his voice.

'No,' she whispered breathlessly. 'Why should you say that?'

'You don't remember? After responding most satisfactorily, you then became so cool that I could only conclude you didn't care for my kisses after all.'

'Oh, that? Yes, I remember.' She lowered her head as her colour heightened at the memory of the way she had revealed her emotions. And as there was no longer any necessity for silence she told him it was because she thought he had kissed her solely for Rosa's benefit.

'Rosa?' He frowned in puzzlement. 'I don't quite understand you, Joanne?'

'Do you remember, Rosa came along?'

'So she did. But what has that to do with my kissing you?' He held her away from him, his frown deepening.

'I thought you knew she was there and had kissed me just for her benefit. You see, Manoel,' she went on hastily as his puzzlement increased, 'I overheard Dona Clementina and your stepfather talking, and I know about the promise you made to your uncle.'

'I see. . . . You listened to their conversation?'

Joanne twisted her hands uncomfortably and then told him how it had happened.

'I know I should have moved away,' she added on a note of contrition, 'but I just had to listen.'

'That was natural, in the circumstances. In any case, you'd have to know some time – now that we're to be married, that is.' A thoughtful pause, and then, 'So you know why I wanted to become engaged?'

'Yes. And I know why you want to marry me.' Unconsciously a little note of depression entered her voice. Yet she was not unhappy, far from it – but if only—

'Do you, Joanne?' Something in the way he said that brought her head up with a jerk. 'But then you thought you knew why I kissed you.'

She quivered under his touch as his fingers caressed her arm.

'Didn't you—? Wasn't it—?'

'I kissed you, my lovely Joanne, because I wanted to, and I'm going to kiss you now for the same reason.'

LYNN was seated before the dressing table when Joanne knocked at her bedroom door.

'Come in.' She turned, smiling, and Joanne looked her over appreciatively.

'Going somewhere?' she inquired, without much expression.

'To the café, with Ricardo.' Twisting round in the chair again, Lynn picked up the comb. Joanne smiled to herself, visualizing the flush that had risen to her friend's cheeks. 'I've been thinking, Joanne, I really should be making a move for home.'

'I've invited you to be my bridesmaid,' exclaimed Joanne in surprise. 'Or have you forgotten? The dressmaker's coming to measure you tomorrow for your dress.'

'I know I promised, Joanne,' hesitantly. 'But I've been here nearly three weeks. I'm a stranger to Manoel and feel I mustn't impose on him like this.'

Ignoring that Joanne said, curiously,

'Do you want to go home?' She came further into the room and sat down on the bed.

'No, not by any means!' The words slipped out, followed by the more softly spoken, 'Ricardo . . .'

'Yes?'

'He – he doesn't like the idea at all – though I said I must go,' she added hastily. 'We shall correspond, of course, and he says he'll come over for a visit very soon.'

'And you'll just sit there, on your own, waiting for this visit?' Watching her friend, and noting her changing expression, Joanne knew that Lynn's thoughts were running on exactly the same lines as her own. Were she to leave Portugal now the affair with Ricardo could easily develop into a pen friendship, and finally come to an end altogether. 'I shouldn't trouble about going home yet awhile,' Joanne advised. 'Or bother your head about Manoel. He said himself that we could expect you to be with us for quite some time.'

'He did?' Lynn blinked at Joanne through the mirror. 'Why should he say a thing like that?'

Joanne laughed.

'It was fairly clear, at the Christmas party, that you and Ricardo were attracted to one another, and as you've been out with him every night since—'

'Not every night!'

Shrugging, Joanne passed that off.

'Stay, Lynn, for just as long as you like. Manoel said at the beginning I must tell you this, and he sincerely meant it.' Absently she picked up a small gilt picture frame from the table beside the bed. Lynn had kept the photograph because her mother was on it ... but so was the boy to whom Lynn had once been engaged. 'You've been a dutiful daughter – oh, I know that any daughter worth her salt would have done the same, and I'm not making a heroine of you. But you did make a sacrifice when you gave Derek up. Don't throw away this second chance of happiness, Lynn, because there's no need now. And you'll never find anyone quite as nice as Ricardo – he's charming, in addition to being extra ordinarily good-looking.' A faint smile hovered on Joanne's lips as her thoughts strayed to those moments of her own uncertainty. She had felt sure her pleasant little emotion of warmth and content had been the first germ of love. At that time, she reflected, the arrogant Dom Manoel had been away out of reach, up on his lofty pedestal from where he had gazed down on her with a mingling of indifference and disdain.

'If you're quite sure he won't mind?' began Lynn. 'I did think I'd look around for a job – if I stayed here, that was.'

Joanne's smile deepened. She had a strong premonition that, should Lynn decide to remain in Portugal, the affair would develop so rapidly that it would not be long before Ricardo proposed.

'Enjoy your stay,' she advised. 'Consider it a holiday for the time being. As I've said, Manoel expects you to prolong your visit.'

After putting the finishing touches to her hair Lynn rose from the stool and stood looking at Joanne for a moment in silence.

'He's a wonderful person,' she said. 'You're very lucky, Joanne.'

'I agree.'

'You gave me to understand that he doesn't love you,' Lynn said awkwardly. 'And I'm sure you should know ... but the way he treats you. ... It *can't* all be for Rosa's benefit!'

Joanne replaced the picture on the table.

'No, Lynn, it can't,' she returned confidently. 'I now believe he cares for me. He did say, quite openly, that he didn't love me, but I'm sure it was only because he thought *I* didn't love *him*.'

'He knows now that you love him?'

Joanne's grey eyes lit with humour.

'He'd be obtuse if he didn't,' she admitted with a little self-conscious laugh. He still had not actually said he loved her, but then Joanne had not seen much of him for the past week. Two days after Christmas he had taken Helena and her children home, and had then gone on down to his other estate in the Algarve, which he visited periodically in order to have business discussions with his manager.

'I'm ever so glad it's turned out all right.' Lynn's voice, warm and sincere, broke into Joanne's musings and she glanced up. 'You haven't yet made your confession?' A statement rather than a question and a rueful shake of Joanne's head was the only answer, though she made a mental resolution to acquaint her fiancé with the truth the moment he returned.

But Joanne did not happen to be in on his return, for she had gone over to Pendela Farm to do a little tidying up – not in the house itself, but outside. For Luis had left some rubbish about and Joanne decided to start a fire and burn it.

Glee had not yet gone back to school after the Christmas holiday and she accompanied Joanne, helping her and becoming decidedly grubby in the process.

'Shall I put these on the fire?' she asked, her arms full of sticks and other rubbish she had collected from around the back of the house.

'Just drop them down; I'll put them on the fire.' Joanne's eyes twinkled with amusement at the picture her niece presented. Truly she should have been a boy – no matter how much Manoel asserted that it would be a waste.

'I've got a secret,' Glee said, on dropping her load. 'And I'm not telling anybody except Uncle Manoel.'

'No?' Joanne picked up a long pole and stirred the fire. 'You won't even tell me?'

Glee shook her head.

'Only Uncle Manoel, and nobody else in the world!'

Joanne did not persisit, considering Glee to be merely teasing her.

'See what's in the shed – but don't pick anything up that's too dirty.'

'Okay,' said Glee blithely, running off in the direction of the shed. 'There's a mouse in there,' she observed a few minutes later on bringing out some old papers. 'Look, it's been chewing these.' They were brown paper bags which had contained corn for the fowls, and should have been destroyed by Luis, and Joanne began putting them on to the fire. And then a white envelope, also partly chewed, caught her eye and she picked it up, a sudden frown appearing as she held it between her fingers, staring at the handwriting.

Her brother. . . . And the date— This would have arrived the day before yesterday. Baffled, Joanne turned it over and over, as if by doing so some explanation would occur to her. All she saw was – 'Miss J. Barrie. . . .' How had this got into the shed? And where was the letter it had contained?

As Joanne told Lynn, all her letters were delivered to the farm, and she collected them herself. Manoel had a key – but no one else. . . . Joanne's eyes glinted. The key of Pendela Farm was kept in a drawer in the small cabinet in the salon. Had someone else been to the farm and picked up this letter? Stupid question, she realized. Of course someone had picked up the letter, because she herself had never set eyes on it.

'Come,' she said to Glee. 'Let's see what else we can find.'

They searched about, with Glee picking up odd bits of straw and wood that lay scattered about the floor, but there was no sign of the letter.

'What are you looking for, Mummy?'

'The letter that was in this envelope. Have you seen it at all, Glee?'

'No . . . the letters go to our farm, though.'

'Usually they do.' Joanne pursed her lips thoughtfully as Glee wandered around, picking up rubbish off the floor. Manoel had never been interested enough to ask about her mail. If he thought of the matter at all he would probably conclude that it came to the Solar de Alvares and that Diego took it up to her immediately it arrived. But Rosa. . . . Could it be that, with her unusual interest in all that concerned Joanne, Rosa had noticed that her letters did not come to the house? That Joanne received letters would be certain, and if they weren't coming to the Solar de Alvares then they must be still going to the farm. Why? That would be a question Rosa would be sure to ask, and once her curiosity was aroused she would have no scruples about investigating the matter for herself. But no, surely even Rosa would not go as far as to take the key, enter her home and pick up one of her letters. 'But who else is there?' murmured Joanne softly.

'What did you say, Mummy?'

'Nothing, Glee dear. Come on, let's tidy out this shed and burn all this rubbish.'

Immediately on their arrival back at the house Joanne sent Glee upstairs to wash and change; then she went in search of Rosa. She was in the small sitting-room, Diego informed Joanne, and as she opened the door and entered the room she realized with a start that Manoel was also there. He stood by the window, his hands thrust into his pockets, listening to all Rosa had to say. At Joanne's entry the Portuguese girl stopped speaking, but Joanne had heard sufficient to convince her that Rosa had already passed on her information to Manoel. Manoel's attention was transferred to Joanne; his hard eyes travelled over her, slowly, the expression in their depths a mingling of bewildered disbelief and contempt. Flushing hotly, Joanne moved further into the room, pushing the door to behind her and at the same time noticing the unmistakable air of triumph about Rosa, who was sitting on the sofa, leaning back, her elegant legs crossed, and one manicured hand resting on the cushion at her side.

Manoel spoke, in tones so soft and dangerous that Joanne's spine tingled in spite of her knowledge that apart from his anger at her deception, she had nothing to fear.

'Perhaps you will tell me, Joanne, why you've been deceiving me all this time?'

Joanne's eyes flickered from Manoel to Rosa, and back again.

'Rosa has told you I'm not a widow?'

'So it's true?' He looked at her incredulously, and Joanne had the impression that although he had just questioned her, he had half expected a denial. 'You've never been married?'

Joanne stood there, clasping her hands, her face as white as her blouse.

'I've never been married, Manoel – and of course I meant to tell you this. However, it's not really important, because Glee—'

'Not important!' He stared speechlessly at her, while Rosa murmured in smooth and even tones,

'You see, Manoel, I was perfectly right in my estimation of this girl's character.'

Her character? Swiftly Joanne glanced from Rosa to Manoel. So. . . . It was not merely that she had posed as a widow—

Turning on Rosa, her eyes blazing, Joanne demanded to

know just what was Rosa's estimation of her character. But the Portuguese girl had no chance to reply, for Manoel was saying, in a dazed sort of way, but with fury in his tones,

'It's not important? You tell me you've never been married – and it's not important. Are you quite shameless!'

Silence – the silence of amazement. Now of course was the time to take warning ... but unfortunately Joanne scarcely heard those cautious whisperings that clamoured for attention. For at the sight of these two watching her, Manoel with fury and contempt and Rosa with triumph, her own eyes kindled dangerously. And as on a previous occasion, when Manoel had treated her to his manner of arrogant superiority, that troublesome streak of obstinacy reared up, dominating her to the exclusion of every other emotion.

This was his opinion of her. Love. ... Joanne's mouth curved bitterly. He had not declared his love, and the reason was not, as she had supposed, that a suitable opportunity had not yet come, but simply because no love existed. For with love came trust, and with trust came the confidence of some quite feasible explanation of everything the loved one did. But Manoel desired no explanation; he was perfectly willing to believe Rosa's accusations, to accept without question the validity of the information she had obviously been waiting to impart to him immediately on his return.

Looking at Rosa, Joanne said quietly,

'Perhaps you'll tell me exactly what you've said to Manoel?'

Rosa shrugged, and said in careless tones,

'I've had my suspicions from the start. And then the other day I happened to come across a letter—'

'You happened to come across it?' interrupted Joanne softly, aware of her fiancé's interest in this interchange between herself and Rosa. 'A letter was stolen from my house. I found the envelope in the shed.'

'So that's where it went. It blew out of my hand.' She sent Joanne an untroubled glance from under her long silken lashes. 'I don't quite know what you mean by stolen. The letter, which I imagine should have been dropped into your letter-box at the farm, was in some bushes in the field. It had apparently been wet through and then dried, for the envelope came off and, as I said, it blew away, and I never saw it again. It was addressed to *Miss* J. Barrie.'

That explanation could be the correct one, Joanne generously conceded. There was no door on the shed and the envelope might have blown inside.

'You knew the letter was mine. Why didn't you give it to me?'

'I would most certainly have done so. But as I've explained, the envelope came off. The letter blew open and I couldn't help reading its contents.'

'How very convenient all this was. The letter in the bushes, the wind blowing it open. . . . .' Joanne was no longer willing to give Rosa the benefit of the doubt. 'A postman usually makes sure the letters are put in the box,' she submitted, and, when no response was forthcoming, 'As you did not consider it your duty to pass on my property you have the advantage of me regarding its contents. Perhaps you'll enlighten me?'

'The letter's here!' Picking it up from the cabinet at his elbow, Manoel flung it across the room. Stooping, Joanne took it from the carpet. Opening it out, she read,

'My dear Joanne,
I'm sorry I haven't written before, but I've been ill for nearly three weeks. That's why I haven't sent you any money for Glee's Christmas present. How is my little daughter?' There followed more questions about Glee and then, 'Life isn't always pleasant with Mavis, and I sometimes wish I'd stayed with you and Glee. Give her a big kiss from her daddy.

Love,

Roger.'

Slowly Joanne folded it up. Damning it most certainly must appear to anyone not in possession of the facts, but as she looked across at Manoel, and saw the contempt and condemnation in his eyes, her chin lifted and she stubbornly refrained from commenting on the contents of the letter in her hand.

'You've nothing to say?' Bitter disillusionment now in Manoel's dark eyes, and for one brief moment Joanne wondered if he cared. But even in her moment of indecision his eyes darkened again with blame and disgust and he turned away, as if he never wanted to set eyes on her again.

Suddenly her sister's remark about the proud boast of the Alvares came to her. What was he thinking? – that Glee had tainted his noble home? She turned, and probably would have left the room, but Rosa's sneering, triumphant face caught her attention and she whipped round. The rein on her fury was released and she told them both what she thought of them.

'And as for you,' she finally cried, tossing her head as she turned to Manoel, 'I always did consider you pompous and proud and conceited! – and I wouldn't marry you now if you went down on your knees and asked me!' She stopped for breath, and noticed the raising of his brows. The noble and aristocratic Dom Manoel Alvares going down on his knees! That was a silly thing for her to say but she went on blindly, her words born of a deeply injured pride, 'You're the most detestable man I've ever met! I thought you really cared for Glee, liked her for herself – but you're so wrapped up in your own superiority and your stupid possessions that you can't get your values straight! Glee's just as good as you are – better, in fact—!' And some mischief suddenly entering into her caused her to add, just for good measure, '—even if I'm not married to her father!' But no sooner had the words left her lips than she regretted them; it was not only that Manoel had actually flinched or that Rosa's sneer had reappeared, but Joanne herself felt thoroughly ashamed of uttering such wild impetuous words.

However, before she could decide what to do the awful silence that had settled on the room was broken by the entrance of Glee. For a brief moment she stood there, her short little dress starched and flouncing, her nose gleaming from the soap she had vigorously used upon it.

'Uncle Manoel – oh, I'm so glad to see you!' Running to him, she grabbed his hand and put it to her cheek in a little habit she had adopted with him recently. Breathlessly Joanne awaited his reaction ... and to her amazement and disbelief he smiled down at the child, and ruffled her hair with his other hand. Rosa stared incredulously, and opened her mouth to speak, but Glee was before her.

'I've got a secret, Uncle Manoel, and I've been waiting a long time to tell you.'

'Glee dear,' said Joanne, in a trembling, yet much quieter tone, 'Uncle Manoel isn't interested in what you have to say. Come—'

'But I've waited a long time,' repeated Glee, 'I can tell you, can't I?'

'Yes, Glee,' he said, his eyes fixed on Joanne's flushed and angry countenance. 'What is it you have to tell me?'

'I know who it was who knocked me down. It was Dona Rosa.'

The slow, heavy tick of the grandfather clock was the only sound in the room for several moments after Glee had made her pronouncement. Rosa's face had gone a sort of sickly yellow; Manoel's was merely a mask.

'Glee—' began Joanne, when Manoel raised a hand.

'That is a very serious thing to say, Glee. Are you quite sure it's true?'

'Of course it isn't true! The child romances all the time; you can't believe a word she says!'

'I found my hair-slide.' Glee looked up at Manoel, her eyes wide and frank. 'I lost my slide that day, and I found it, fastened in Dona Rosa's lamp. And I remember now that it was a black car,' she added, twisting round to look up at Rosa. 'You said it wasn't, but it was.'

'You said it wasn't?' Frowning, Manoel transferred his gaze to his cousin. If he had any further doubt it was swept away by the guilt on her face.

Leave them to it, decided Joanne, glancing disdainfully from one to the other and, beckoning to Glee, who came to her at once, she and the child went out, and up to their own private rooms.

Lynn was there, sitting comfortably on the couch, reading. She raised her head and smiled as Joanne and Glee entered the room, but instantly the smile faded as she noted Joanne's expression.

'Is anything wrong?'

'Everything's wrong!' Joanne sat down and snatched up a magazine that lay on the chair. But of course she didn't attempt to read it and after a moment she tossed it down again, and as Lynn was obviously waiting for some explanation she proceeded to tell her all that had happened.

For a while after she had finished speaking her friend could only stare in a sort of dumb amazement.

'Joanne, are you quite mad! You've allowed Manoel to believe Glee's ...? Really, you must be out of your mind. Why didn't you tell him she was your niece?'

'Because he condemned me out of hand, that's why!'

With a firm decisive movement Lynn put down her book and rose from the couch.

'I'm going right down there and putting things straight! This attitude of obstinacy's absolutely ridiculous!'

'Don't you dare, Lynn! If Manoel likes to think that of me, then let him! Besides, it doesn't matter, because I've told him I'm not marrying him.'

'You've thrown him over?' Lynn's face went pale. 'Joanne, you can't do this; it's your whole life's happiness you're throwing away!'

'I have my pride.' Joanne's mouth was quivering in spite of herself, and the tears were pricking the backs of her eyes. 'If he doesn't trust me, then how could we ever have been happy? No, Lynn, I'm going home, and – and I'll s-soon forget Manoel Alvares and this place. I'll f-forget in n-no time at all!'

A great sigh left Lynn's lips.

'I'll make you a drink of tea,' she said practically, and went off to fill the kettle.

'Mummy . . . are we leaving here?'

Joanne turned; Glee was sitting on the rug, looking up at her, her little face puckered and her eyes bewildered and questioning.

'Yes, Glee. It's better for us to go home to our own country. You'll see Auntie Chris and Uncle Miles,' she added, forcing a smile for the child's benefit. 'And you'll see your daddy. That will be better than staying here, won't it?'

'I won't see Uncle Manoel, though.' Glee shook her head. 'Next to you I love Uncle Manoel best in the whole world.'

'No, Glee dear, your daddy is the one you love most.'

'Uncle Manoel's like my daddy – and he loves me, because he said so.'

'He said so?' Joanne looked down at her in puzzlement.

'I asked him if he loved me and he said yes.' Her thoughts switched, as they often did. 'Do you think he'll be very cross with Dona Rosa for knocking me down with her car?'

'Perhaps, Glee. Why wouldn't you tell me about it? Why did you have to save it for Uncle Manoel?'

'Because he asked me – two times – if I could remember what kind of a car it was that knocked me down. He said if ever I remembered I must tell him – so I did.'

Lynn returned with the kettle and soon they were drinking the tea she had made.

'It was a disgusting trick of Rosa's, to take one of your letters. I wonder what put the idea into her head?'

'It was a shot in the dark, I think. She's known from the first that there was some mystery, and as I told you, she intended making inquiries about me when she went to England. She was prevented, as you know, but when Manoel announced the date for the wedding she became desperate. The actual idea of intercepting one of my letters could have come from Dona Clementina,' Joanne added as the idea occurred to her. She looked resignedly at her friend. 'I didn't stand a chance with the two of them.'

A sigh of sheer exasperation escaped Lynn.

'You have truth on your side, Joanne. That's sufficient.'

'You think I should go to Manoel and tell him the truth?'

'I don't think – I'm sure!'

'Well, I'm not going to,' returned Joanne obstinately. 'He's listened to Rosa—'

'Rosa had the letter,' Lynn reminded her. 'He didn't just take her word without giving you a hearing.'

'He didn't give me a hearing, Lynn. He didn't want my explanation.'

'From what you tell me you didn't offer one,' commented Lynn with a dry edge to her voice.

'He should have known I wasn't like that – should have trusted me.'

Leaning across Joanne, Lynn took the letter from the table and read it again.

'If he loves you, he'd naturally see red on reading this. You must admit it does give a devilishly wrong impression.' Lynn could not help laughing, and Joanne threw her an indignant glance.

'If he loved me he'd trust me – and wouldn't believe a word of that letter.'

'I give up!' Lynn tossed the letter on to the table. 'I daresay you'll come to your senses in your own good time.'

'I'm not going to marry him.'

'Aren't I going to be a bridesmaid, then?' Glee asked, and Joanne saw that she was very close to tears. 'I want you to marry Uncle Manoel, and I want to stay here for always.'

'You're going to stay here for always,' declared Lynn. 'Because if your stupid aunt doesn't make up her quarrel with Uncle Manoel, then your Auntie Lynn will take a hand.'

'If you interfere,' warned Joanne, looking straight at her, 'I'll never speak to you again!' And, at that moment, she really meant what she said.

CHAPTER TEN

HOWEVER, it was not long before Joanne's state of mind underwent a complete change and she was able to view the situation from the angle at which it had been presented to Manoel by his cousin. To come home, be told that the letter was addressed to *Miss* Barrie, and then be confronted by the irrefutable evidence that Glee's father was not only very much alive, but also corresponding with Joanne, and even sending her his love, must have come as a shock so stunning that, for a while, Manoel's customary ease of clear thinking must have been impaired. Had she, Joanne, come upon him later the result might have been different. Having had time to think, and perhaps discover some flaw in the picture Rosa had presented to him, he would not have condemned Joanne out of hand, but would have required a statement from Joanne herself before passing judgment upon her. Coming swiftly on this more reasonable view of her fiancé's behaviour was the admission that her own conduct had been both foolish and inexcusable: foolish because she had let pass the opportunity of turning the tables on her enemy, and inexcusable because she had deliberately allowed Manoel to remain misinformed regarding the true position. The more she dwelt on her own culpability – even while at the same time reflecting dismally on the disparaging remarks she had made about his character – the more she began to wonder if she had placed herself quite beyond his pardon.

She managed to avoid him until dinner. During the meal several frigid glances came her way, but whenever possible Joanne avoided his eyes. Rosa sat there, her hatred and anger seeming to pervade the whole room, and Joanne knew there had been serious trouble between them over the question of Glee's accident.

When the meal was finished Manoel said curtly, 'We'll have coffee in my room, Joanne. I want to speak to you.'

Although she wished for nothing more than to clear up the whole miserable business, she took fright on noticing the severity of his expression and said hastily,

'I'm rather tired . . . perhaps in the morning . . . ?'

'Now!' he snapped, and went out, expecting her to follow.

Rosa stood up and left the table; her dark eyes swept insultingly over Joanne's slender figure.

'You look quite pale,' she sneered. 'Aren't you feeling well?' Joanne ignored that and Rosa went on, cool triumph in her eyes, 'I've been endeavouring for weeks to think of a way of unmasking you, for you were making a complete fool of Manoel.'

'So you made an unlawful entry into my house and stole my letter?' The contempt in Joanne's voice registered and Rosa's face darkened with anger.

'Had I been able to visit my friends in England I'd have taken the opportunity of making some inquiries about you. With the postponement of my visit this was the only way.'

'So you do admit taking the letter from my house?'

'Yes,' was the surprising confession. 'Your letters never came here, and for some time I've been puzzled about that. It was obvious you had something to hide, and naturally I concluded information could be gleaned from your letters—And I certainly did glean information,' she added, 'because I learned at once that you'd never been married.'

'That must have afforded you immense satisfaction,' commented Joanne, imperturbably folding her napkin and slipping it into the ring. Her calm manner struck Rosa forcibly and she regarded her in puzzlement for a while before saying,

'It was entirely for Manoel's sake, and fortunately it's brought him to his senses. He knows now what you are, and so it seems – *Miss* Joanne Barrie – that you'll be the one leaving the Solar de Alvares, and not me, after all.'

'I don't think so, Rosa.' Standing up, Joanne faced the girl who, from the moment of their first meeting, had shown her nothing but open hostility. 'You've wasted your time, I'm afraid, because your little scheme has failed.'

Rosa glanced sharply at her, a frown appearing on her brow.

'Surely you're not supposing he still wants to marry you?'

'Did Manoel tell you he didn't now want to marry me?' inquired Joanne curiously, for the moment diverted from what she had meant to say.

The dark lashes fluttered down and Rosa thought carefully before she spoke.

'Not in so many words ... but it's obvious, isn't it? An Alvares could never marry anyone with a stain like that on her character.'

Joanne's eyes kindled dangerously, and her anger rose to form a tightness in her throat that made speech impossible for a second or two. An Alvares. ... Who did he think he was—? Just as that obstinate streak threatened to take possession she pulled herself up. Unless she practised caution she would find herself walking out on Manoel ... and bitterly regretting it for the rest of her days.

'When he hears what I have to say I feel sure Manoel won't want to break our engagement.' Despite her outward confidence, she knew a tremor of fear. Manoel could not be blamed if he refused to forgive her. But his one object was to get Rosa out of his house, she instantly reminded herself. Yes, he would still want to marry her, once he knew Glee was only her niece, Joanne felt she need have no doubts about that.

'What have you to say?' Rosa's eyes glinted with amusement. 'You can't possibly have any explanation for – Glee!'

That choking sensation in her throat again. Joanne determinedly kept her temper.

'It so happens, Rosa, that both you and Manoel are under a misapprehension about Glee. She's my brother's child.'

'Your—?' The amusement was wiped from Rosa's eyes. She stared at Joanne in utter disbelief. 'Your brother's child? Do you expect to get away with a story like that?'

'It's the truth. The letter you stole was from Roger, my brother. Glee came to us – to my mother and sister and me – when Roger's wife died—'

'Why, then, the necessity for assuming the role of widow?' interrupted Rosa sceptically.

'I had a reason for that.'

'Glee calls you Mummy,' Rosa reminded her in the same sceptical tones. 'What explanation can there be for that?'

Joanne told her, though only as briefly as possible. She also told Rosa how she came to be the one to have Glee, and even explained why she was reluctant to let the child go back to her father and stepmother. But when she had finished Rosa was shaking her head, apparently determined to disbelieve the story, and Joanne began to regret having taken the trouble to relate it to her.

'Are you expecting a tale like that to carry any weight with Manoel?' she asked with a lift of her brows.

'I have in my possession Glee's birth certificate. That should suffice.'

Confounded by this news, the only thing Rosa could find to say was,

'In that case, you'll be sending Glee back to her father?'

'It is my intention to keep Glee with me.'

'You actually expect Manoel to make himself responsible for your brother's child?'

'I believe he will do so.' But would he? Sudden fear entered into Joanne. This question of Glee had troubled her whenever she had thought about an eventual marriage for herself. And hadn't Chris doubted the willingness of any man to take Glee, knowing she was only Joanne's niece, and that her father was still living?

'Then you're more optimistic than I would be in your position. I can't conceive how you could expect Manoel to have Glee. Your brother's married – I gathered from the letter – so naturally Manoel will expect the child to go to her father and stepmother.'

A little pale now, Joanne said doggedly,

'I'm sure he'll want to keep her.'

'You're not sure at all, are you?' she said gloatingly. 'In fact you're fast becoming convinced that he definitely won't take Glee.' She laughed on seeing the consternation enter Joanne's eyes. 'You're in a bit of a quandary, aren't you? Tell Manoel the truth and he'll insist on your sending the child away; let him believe she's yours and he won't marry you at all—'

'Joanne!' Manoel's imperative voice interrupted her and Joanne went swiftly from the room. He stood at the end of the hall, by the open door of his room. 'I told you to come here!' Turning on his heel, he went back into the room; Joanne followed, closing the door behind her and standing by it, looking across at her fiancé, who was now seated at the small table, his coffee cup in front of him. 'Where have you been?' he demanded, and then, indicating the chair opposite to him, 'Sit down.'

'I was talking to Rosa,' she answered quietly, and poured herself some coffee. 'Manoel, I'm very sorry for all those awful things I said to you. I didn't mean them.'

He eyed her darkly, his mouth compressed and his jaw set in a tight and rigid line.

'It was fortunate for you that Rosa was there. You have things to learn, apparently, and one of them is that I don't allow anyone to speak to me like that – not even my wife!'

'You still want to marry me, then?' Even though he had not yet learned the truth about Glee, she thought, watching him curiously.

Manoel's expression changed. Gone was the harshness and anger Joanne had encountered on entering the room, and a strange hurt took their place. He spoke to her quietly, and Joanne felt that if it had been his original intention to upbraid her he had now changed his mind. It was as if he had swiftly recognized the situation and decided there was nothing to be gained by adopting an attitude of angry reproach.

'We're engaged, Joanne. Certainly I want to marry you.'

This left Joanne speechless. Was this obsession to rid himself of Rosa so strong that he would marry Joanne, even while believing she had a 'past'? 'I'm extremely disappointed in you,' he went on, still in the same quiet tones, 'for the way in which you've deceived me. On thinking the matter over I can understand your wanting to be thought of as a widow, and I'm willing to make allowances for your earlier deceit. But latterly, when you knew we were to be married— You must have realized you couldn't appear in church as a widow?'

'Yes, of course I did – and I've been trying to tell you, Manoel, but I was . . . afraid.'

He considered this, and in the belief that there was much more to it than the mere confession that she was not a widow, he thought he understood.

'It would be difficult for you to approach me, I admit—' He broke off, glancing at her in bewilderment and shaking his head. 'I would have had to know some time.'

'I intended telling you immediately on your return.' She remained staggered at his willingness to marry her while still under the illusion that Glee was hers, and she hesitated, recalling Rosa's firm assertion that Manoel would refuse to have Glee, once he knew there was no obstacle in the way of her return to her father. She glanced across at him, her mind in a state of terrible uncertainty. He looked tired, she thought, and dispirited – and that was not like Manoel. But he had received a severe shock, and it had left its mark. She must tell him the truth, she decided, for surely he would not let Glee go to parents who did not want her.

'Manoel,' she began, 'it's not as bad as you think – oh, I know I've done wrong—'

'I couldn't take it in, even though I had the letter in my hand, and Rosa had said it was addressed to *Miss* Barrie.' He regarded her like a man dazed. 'It just didn't seem to fit *you* – not as I had come to know you and at first I actually deceived myself by assuming there was some mistake, by thinking that Glee must be someone else's child. But of course I was merely clutching at a straw; there's the resemblance, for one thing, and in any case, you would be most unlikely to saddle yourself with a child who wasn't yours. No one in their right mind would.'

Saddle . . . no one in their right mind would. . . .

'You'd never take anyone else's child?' She seemed no more than a child herself, looking across at him, quite unconscious of the plea in her voice. Manoel heard it – and mistook its meaning.

'I still want to marry you, Joanne, and naturally I shall take your child.'

Joanne helped herself to sugar, and slowly stirred her coffee. What should she do? As things were, Manoel was willing to have Glee; he cared for her, and he would be a father to her. Here, in the lovely Portuguese mansion, she would have a good life. Should Joanne reveal the truth, then she would be faced with the terrible decision of parting from Glee or parting from Manoel. Her love for Glee was strong; her love for Manoel stronger. But her decision would not be so simple as that, for there was the child herself. Could she, Joanne, place her own happiness first and hand Glee over to a couple who did not want her? – and who in fact were not even happily married, from all accounts? No, she would not condemn Glee to life in that kind of environment. Here at the Solar de Alvares she had fitted in; everyone loved her, from the servants in the house to the workers in the vineyards. Even the stolid Diego had fallen victim to her charms. As for Manoel himself . . . hadn't he told Glee he loved her? But if he loved her, then perhaps. . . . What should she do? Joanne asked herself again. The deception could continue for a while, she felt sure, but the day must dawn when Manoel learned who Glee really was. But if by that time he had come to love her, then he would not hesitate to let her have her own way over Glee. *If* by then he loved her? Recalling how he had said that love might enter their relationship, Joanne made her decision. Manoel was willing to take Glee, so she would leave it at that.

They talked for a while, with an element of reserve ever present, which under the circumstances was only natural, but no real tension was felt by Joanne until Manoel forbade her ever to communicate with Glee's father again. She made the promise, mentally noting two things she must do: write to Roger explaining the situation and asking him not to get in touch again until she gave him permission to do so, and tell Glee she must not talk about her daddy unless they were alone. The first request would be carried out . . . the second would be a matter of luck. However, Glee had been away from her father so long that he was fast becoming a nebulous figure, and in fact Glee only talked about him when Joanne read his letters to her, or when she herself read the notes he enclosed. In the absence of letters from her father it would be unlikely that Glee would talk about him at all.

To Joanne's surprise Manoel suggested a walk before they went to bed, and he seemed more relaxed when they were outside, though at times he seemed a long way from her, his thoughts deep, and private. They sat on a seat under a tree, for the night was pleasantly warm with a cloud blanket keeping in the heat of a day which had been unusually hot for the time of the year. To Joanne's surprise he took her hand, and there was a strange gentleness in his touch. She just had to say,

'Manoel . . . I don't understand. Aren't you very angry?'

He turned from his contemplation of the illuminated fountain in the middle of the lake.

'Why did you shield Rosa over the accident?' he asked, ignoring her question.

'There didn't seem anything to be gained by telling you,' she answered, surprised by his change of the subject.

'That's not all of it. Kindly give me a fuller explanation, Joanne.'

'She said she'd deny it,' Joanne submitted after a long moment of indecision. 'And I didn't think you would accept my word against hers.'

'Why?' he asked simply, and she went on to explain that she was under the impression he and Rosa were engaged to be married.

'Ah, yes, you did think that once. I remember your telling me.' His eyes wandered to the fountain again and he fell silent. What was he thinking? Perhaps, she mused disconsolately, he was wondering about Glee, and about Joanne's age when she was born. How right her mother had been when she prophesied that Glee would some day cause her a great deal of embarrassment! 'She said she'd deny it?' Manoel spoke softly, reflecting on his words. 'Nevertheless, you did shield her, for although she might have denied it your word would have carried more conviction, being true. She on the other hand made no attempt to shield you.' Joanne remained silent, for indeed there was nothing she could find to say to that. 'I suppose this is part of the reason I'm not angry,' he added, almost to himself. 'I do abhor tale-carrying.'

After a little while he suggested they go back to the house, and as they turned to retrace their steps he took hold of her and drew her to him. Although more himself he still seemed rather dazed, but what puzzled Joanne was the way he appeared to be suffering some great hurt. It must be her imagination, she concluded, for he could not be hurt unless he loved her. Disappointed, yes, but not hurt. And yet she said impulsively, the words being strangely drawn from her, almost against her will,

'I'm so sorry, Manoel, for everything I've done.' He would not know the real meaning of those words, of course, and this was manifested in the slight stiffening of his body against hers.

'From tonight, Joanne, we'll not talk about it.'

'No.' The tiny break in her voice softened him and he bent and kissed her on the lips.

'There's a new life beginning for us both,' he said gently. 'And I'm sure it will be a good life.'

When they reached home he kissed her again, then bade her good night.

'Good night, Manoel.' She smiled at him, and ran upstairs. At the top she turned to look down; he was still standing there, staring into space.

Later that night, sitting up in bed with a book, yet unable to read any more than she could sleep, Joanne pondered on her fiancé's acceptance of the situation. And the more she pondered the more convinced she became that there was something she did not understand. Manoel wanted nothing so much as to be released from that old promise, and this he had contrived by placing Rosa in a position in which she would leave his house of her own accord. But any woman would have served his purpose. Besides, he was handsome and rich, had about the most magnificent *palacete* in the whole of the Douro district, and therefore could have had his pick of the daughters of the Portuguese nobility.

And yet he had chosen her, Joanne, taking Glee too who, so he believed, was her child born out of wedlock. He did not seem to care about the gossip that must inevitably ensue. His mother and stepfather, his sisters and brother ... his friends and the vast army of employees....

Yes, there certainly was something Joanne did not understand.

'I'm glad the wedding's on again.' Lynn surveyed herself in the long mirror in Joanne's bedroom. Her dress of flowing lilac velvet was being deftly moulded to her waist by the dressmaker, whose assistant was standing by handing her the pins. 'I like myself, Joanne,' she added, laughing.

'It certainly suits you.' Joanne stood there, surveying her admiringly. 'Ricardo's really going to fall for you in that.'

'Wasn't it good of Manoel to invite him? He seems to think of everything. He's kind, Joanne.'

Joanne bit her lip. Kind, thoughtful, generous ... but still Dom Manoel Alvares, proud scion of a noble Portuguese family. Moving to the window, Joanne gazed down, over the magnificent grounds with their fountains and statuary, their miniature cascades and shining lakes, and her eyes were shadowed and pensive.

Something had crept into her relationship with Manoel and there was an atmosphere of strain between them whenever they found themselves alone. Was it Glee? Would she be a constant reminder to him of Joanne's 'lapse' as Rosa would have termed it? If this were so, then Manoel would never come to love her – and if he never loved her how was she ever to make her confession about Glee? And the confession would have to be made some time.

'*Senhora*. . . .' The dressmaker's voice brought Joanne round and she surveyed Lynn's dress, beautifully moulded to her figure and flowing out from the waist down. 'This is very good, yes?'

'Perfect.'

'And the back, *senhora*?'

Lynn turned round and Joanne nodded.

'And now it's your turn,' said Lynn. 'I'm dying to see your dress now the alterations are nearly finished.'

Joanne's dress was very old, having been the wedding-dress of Manoel's great-grandmother. Made of the finest lace, it had been the work of dozens of nuns, working every stitch by hand, often by candlelight. It was the most exquisite creation she had ever seen, and when told by Manoel that she was to wear it Joanne had been both thrilled and honoured. But now. . . .

'Joanne – oh, you look like a princess!'

It was true; Joanne did look like some proud young princess as she stood there, regarding herself in the mirror, the dressmaker kneeling to adjust the hem.

'Mummy!' Glee flew into the room in her usual whirlwind fashion. 'You look beautiful! I didn't know the dressmaker was here. Am I going to try my dress on? And what about Leonor and Filipa – they should be here, shouldn't they? – to have their fittings? Are you having it right to the floor? Auntie Lynn, have you had your fitting?' Glee sat down on a chair and looked interestedly at the dressmaker's assistant as she passed the pins, one at a time, to the woman on the floor.

'Well, thank heaven you had to stop for breath!' exclaimed Lynn, who was now attired in her ordinary clothes. 'Yes, you're going to try your dress on. No, Leonor and Filipa are not trying on theirs today. Mummy is having her dress down to the floor – and I've had my fitting. Now, would you like to start again?'

Glee grinned and her grey eyes twinkled with mischief.

'I know I ask too many questions. Auntie Chris used to say so. I'm glad Auntie Chris and Uncle Miles are coming to the wedding. I haven't seen them for such a long time.'

What would Chris say to the deception? Joanne wondered with a tiny sigh. There seemed to be so many complications.

'*Senhora* – please move round, just a little.'

Joanne did as she was requested. All this was going on, and yet through her subconscious the words kept repeating themselves, 'The wedding will not take place'.

So many difficulties. . . . And the growing conviction that she should think again. Could she adapt herself to this exalted position without the love of her husband to help her? – and with the shadow of Glee always between them?

She had been quite happy and confident until that conversation with Rosa, she reflected with a sudden creasing of her forehead. Yes, it was Rosa who had caused this uncertainty, this doubt to enter into her.

It was a few days ago; most of Rosa's things had gone the previous day, and Diego was putting a suitcase in her car when Joanne entered the house from the garden. Rosa was coming downstairs, carrying her handbag, and a coat over her arm.

'So we say good-bye.' The usual sneer curled Rosa's lips and her eyes were filled with bitter jealousy and hate. 'I never believed Manoel could go to these lengths, could be so rash. But he'll soon wake up and realize his mistake. He'll realize it every time he sets eyes on your child!' Joanne blinked at her, for she suddenly knew that Rosa was actually deriving satisfaction from the idea of Glee's becoming a barrier between Manoel and his wife. 'You're a brave woman, Joanne, I'll give you that!'

Joanne had been trembling from head to foot as she watched Rosa drive away along the wide tree-lined avenue leading to the road. And all colour must have left her face, for Manoel, coming in a moment later, had concernedly asked if she were feeling ill.

And in a fleeting moment of panic Joanne had opened her mouth to tell her fiancé the truth, for the expression on his face was tender, and his touch had been a gentle caress as he took her arm, insisting she sit down and have a drink of wine. But the words died on her lips as she recalled Manoel's saying that no one in his right mind would saddle himself with someone else's child.

'*Senhora*, if you will turn again, please.' The faintly apologetic request of the dressmaker brought Joanne back to the present, and she turned round, so that the woman could fix the train to her satisfaction.

'It's beautiful,' said Lynn admiringly when at last the woman rose from her knees. 'You've nearly finished it?'

'Many hours yet. The work – it must be done very slow, and very fine, to match the other, you see.'

'Thank you,' murmured Joanne, on being helped to take off the dress. 'You're very clever, because it required a good deal of alteration.'

'It is my business, *senhora*. I do for all the rich people in this district.'

For once Glee managed to keep still as, a few minutes later, she was being fitted. Her dress was a small edition of Lynn's, as were Filipa's and Leonor's, and Glee looked rather angelic as she smiled at herself in the mirror.

'I'm glad Auntie Lynn's being the chief bridesmaid, because now we don't have an argument.'

'There wouldn't have been an argument,' said Joanne. 'Leonor's the eldest, so she would have been the chief bridesmaid.'

'Can I go down and show Uncle Manoel?' asked Glee when the woman informed Joanne that she had finished her work on the dress.

'No; he won't want to be bothered with you.'

However, a week later, when the dresses were finished and Helena brought her children for their final try-on, Helena herself suggested that they should all go down and show the dresses to her brother.

'Oo-h, good!' exclaimed Glee. 'I'll bet Uncle Manoel will think we all look beautiful!'

'Coming?' Helena smiled at her future sister-in-law. 'Let's see what Manoel has to say about them.'

'I'll be down in a few minutes.'

Left alone, Joanne sighed. She experienced no thrill at the idea of going down to see what Manoel thought about the children's dresses. As for her own dress, she had even less interest in that. During the past week it had become more and more difficult not to go to Manoel and call the wedding off, for the coolness between them had increased tenfold, and Joanne could find no reason for it other than that Manoel was by Glee's presence being continually reminded that the woman he was about to marry was not chaste – or so he believed. That Joanne herself could have been blamed for the mounting tension had not for one moment occurred to her.

What would he say if she announced her intention of breaking the engagement? Joanne trembled at the thought . . . yet she trembled even more when she contemplated the future.

At last she went downstairs; excited voices drifted to her from the half open door of the salon as she reached the bottom of the stairs and made her way along the hall towards it.

'Uncle Manoel, aren't we all beautiful?'

'I've answered that question three times already.'

A chuckle from Glee.

'Do you think Leonor's should be a bit shorter?' from Filipa, on a faintly anxious note. 'She might trip over it, and fall down in church.'

'That would be funny!'

'Glee, you have a most perverted sense of humour!'

'What's that, Uncle Manoel?'

'You're wicked!'

Reaching the door, Joanne stood for a moment, most reluctant to enter. For she knew instinctively that a coldness would come over her fiancé the moment their eyes met. So she hesitated, savouring for a while this most attractive mood of his, even though she could only do it from the outside, and alone.

'You don't really think I'm wicked,' returned Glee in an artful tone she had found very effective whenever she particularly wanted to get her own way with Manoel. 'You don't, do you? Because if you did you'd be cross.'

'And if he was cross he'd smack you,' put in Filipa.

'Uncle Manoel won't smack her until he's really her uncle,' interposed Leonor, 'because if you're no relation you can't.'

'Uncle Manoel is my relation.'

'Not until he marries your mummy.'

'Then your mummy'll be your aunt,' said Filipa in some bewilderment. She looked at her sister, and they both laughed. Helena did, too, but Glee was saying seriously,

'Yes – but she's my aunt already. Uncle Manoel, shall I have to call her Aunt after she's married?'

Joanne moved swiftly, her fear almost choking her.

Manoel was speaking.

'No, Glee, you'll still call her Mummy.'

'But she's my aunt, not my—'

'Glee dear—'

'Mummy. . . .' Glee turned to her, 'aren't you really my aunt?'

'No – no – that is— Glee, you must come up and take off your dress. You'll be getting it creased.'

'Creased?' It was Helena who spoke, appearing rather surprised, as well she might, for Glee was merely standing there, not even touching her dress with her hands. 'How can she get it creased?'

'No – well, that was rather silly of me. But I want to take it off. . . .' Joanne caught Manoel's stare. He was looking most oddly at her, and she supposed her appearance had something to do with it, for she knew the colour had left her face. 'Come, Glee.'

'All right – but you are my aunt, aren't you?' No answer

from Joanne and Glee persisted, 'Aren't you really my Auntie Joanne?' She turned to Manoel. 'She is,' she told him cheerfully. 'My real mummy's dead.'

A profound silence settled on the room. Joanne swallowed hard and tried to speak, but with Manoel looking at her like that it was quite impossible for her to do so.

'Joanne,' he said slowly, unbelievingly, 'you haven't answered Glee.'

'I – I—' Whether it was the strain of the past weeks, the relief of knowing everything was cleared up, or the knowledge that this was the end as far as she and Manoel were concerned Joanne could not have said, but to her utter dismay she burst into tears.

'Helena, will you please take the children out?' Manoel's low and authoritative tones reminded Joanne of his efficient handling of another situation – when she had come to him for help.

'Of course, Manoel. Glee, too?'

'Yes. Glee, go along with Aunt Helena. Your – mummy and I want to talk quietly together.'

'But my mummy's crying. I can't leave her.'

'I'll take care of her. You go along with Aunt Helena.'

'Mummy—'

'Do as I say, please, Glee.' Manoel's voice was still tolerant, but firm.

The other children had already left the room and Helena was at the door, waiting for Glee. She hesitated a moment longer, glancing from her aunt to Manoel. Then she noticed the sternness in his eyes and instantly obeyed him.

Silence again. Joanne at last managed to lift her face, and meet her fiancé's gaze.

'I'm sorry I lied, but I knew you wouldn't let her stay, and – and Manoel, I c-can't let her go back to my brother. You see, he's married again, and—'

'So Glee *is* your niece.'

'Yes. Her mother died when she was a baby.' She found a handkerchief and dried her eyes. 'It must be the strain,' she said apologetically, screwing her handkerchief into a tight little ball. 'I can't give Glee up Manoel, so – so the w-wedding will have to be c-called off.'

His eyes flickered strangely.

'Perhaps, Joanne, you'll explain everything to me. I feel I can guess much, but why you began this deception in the first place I simply can't fathom. If Glee wasn't yours, then you had no need to pose as a widow.'

And so Joanne was faced with the embarrassing task of telling Manoel that he had himself been the indirect cause of it all. She then went on to explain how it was that Glee had first begun to call her Mummy.

'You ridiculous child!' he exclaimed when she had finished. 'What a tangle you got yourself into! Why, in heaven's name, didn't you clear it all up before now?'

'I wanted to tell you about Glee – that day when Rosa told you some of it. But you said definitely you wouldn't let me keep her unless she was my own child, so I had to let you go on thinking she was mine.'

'I said—?' He stared at her, a frown on his dark face. 'What are you talking about?'

She began to explain, but she had not gone very far when he interrupted her.

'Did you have to take it quite so literally?'

'You didn't mean it?' She stared at him in disbelief. 'But you definitely said—'

'I certainly never said you couldn't keep Glee, my silly little love. Your memory's at fault.'

My ... love. Dazed, she took a faltering step towards him, even the urgent question of Glee's future forgotten.

'Manoel. ...' Her lovely eyes, still swollen from her weeping, searched his face with a sort of eager desperation. 'Manoel, why do you want to marry me?'

He opened his mouth to say something, then stopped. A hint of amusement entered his dark eyes as at length he said,

'Did you never think to ask yourself why I should still want to marry you, believing Glee to be yours?'

'I did consider it very strange,' she admitted, 'for you

could have had someone much better than I, someone of your own cl—'

Swiftly Manoel crossed the room and Joanne was seized so roughly that the rest of her sentence died on her lips.

'Don't you dare say a thing like that! It's my future wife you're talking about!' And after giving her a little shake he handled her far more gently, and his kiss could leave her in no doubt at all as to the reason why he wanted to marry her. Nevertheless, he whispered, his lips touching her cheek, 'At first, sweetheart, I was concerned only in getting out of that promise I so rashly made to my uncle, but when I asked you to marry me, I knew I was very near to caring.'

'You said you didn't love me,' she reminded him seriously.

'Only because I felt sure you didn't return it. A man doesn't declare his love until he has at least some small indication that he'll not suffer a rebuff. I had no wish to hear you scorn my love.'

She laughed softly then.

'A rebuff . . . you had nothing to fear, because I knew I loved you. But even if I hadn't,' she added on a graver note, 'I would never have said anything horrid to you, Manoel. You should have known that.'

'I should—?' He held her away, his expression a mingling of censure and amusement. 'Perhaps you'll tell me how I should have known a thing like that? – when you've done little else but say horrid things to me almost from the moment we met!'

'That's an exaggeration!' she retorted, though she did have the grace to blush. 'It was only now and then.'

'Well, it had better not be now and then in future!' To the mock warning in his eyes Joanne responded meekly,

'No, Manoel. I'll be a most submissive and respectful wife.' The irrepressible quiver in her voice was not lost on him and he gave her another little shake.

'I'll see that you are!' But his actions belied the threat in his tone, for he took her gently to him and held her lovingly.

'Manoel,' she said after a long while, 'there's something I

don't understand.'

'Yes, my darling, what is it?'

'Lately ... you've been so cold to me, and I began to think it was Glee—'

'I've been cold!' he cut in indignantly. 'You, Joanne, have been like an iceberg!'

'Me? You're blaming me?' she asked in disbelief.

'I certainly am! But I can forgive you now that I understand. You see, darling, you had all this on your mind; subconsciously you were fast acquiring a guilt complex over Glee – and this would in its turn produce inhibitions. You couldn't be free with me, and naturally I was affected by your coolness.' He stopped, shrugging. 'My pride, I suppose. I wanted to retaliate, and so we had this vicious circle, with the position worsening as time went on.' He held her tenderly; she lifted her face and he saw the look of sweet contentment there. 'Thank heaven for Glee,' he whispered fervently, and bent to kiss her lips.

FREE!

Harlequin Romance Catalogue

Here is a wonderful opportunity to read many of the Harlequin Romances you may have missed.

The HARLEQUIN ROMANCE CATALOGUE lists hundreds of titles which possibly are no longer available at your local bookseller. To receive your copy, just fill out the coupon below, mail it to us, and we'll rush your catalogue to you!

Following this page you'll find a sampling of a few of the Harlequin Romances listed in the catalogue. Should you wish to order any of these immediately, kindly check the titles desired and mail with coupon.

HRS 121

Have You Missed Any of These
Harlequin Romances?

Have You Missed Any of These

Harlequin Romances?